THE SILVER FLUTE

THE SILVER FLUTE

LIDA LARRIMORE

GROSSET & DUNLAP
NEW YORK

FOR
BOBBY
*who closed the hatch
and took the ladder away.*

Part One

CHAPTER I

I

THE town hall clock struck briskly, seven ringing notes. Barbara roused in her low carved bed and drowsily opened her eyes. She knew, without remembering why, that it was a happy day. The sunshine against the ceiling, the wind in the willows, the autumn air, fragrant with bonfire smoke and the salty tang of the sea, all held a special promise. What was it? And then she remembered. This was her birthday. To-day she was eighteen years old.

Lying there, her brown hair tumbled against the pillow, her brown eyes bright with pleasure, she saw the happy day unfold. At breakfast there would be presents from Father and the children. They never could bear to wait until later in the day. Father, she thought with a tender smile and a sudden soft little sigh, was worse about hating to wait for things than Kit or Gay or Jamie. In spite of a grown-up daughter, Father was such a child!

Mr. Tubbs, the postman, would bring her godfather's gift. That, every birthday, was exciting—

a gift from someone she hadn't seen since she was
a baby being christened and whom, of course, she
couldn't remember at all. Stephen Drake—"Uncle
Stephen." His taste in gifts was charming. But
he wasn't exactly a friendly person. He never answered her " Thank-you " notes or the cards she
sent him at Christmas.

And she was going on a picnic, a very exclusive
picnic, just she and Bruce and a basket of lunch in
Bruce's rattle-trap car. Barbara smiled, a gay little
smile that woke a sleeping dimple. She knew why
Bruce had suggested a picnic for her birthday. He
was conspiring with Father and the children. They
wanted her party to-night to be a complete surprise.

But it wouldn't be—quite. She knew there was
to be dancing. She had heard Father tell Manuel
to bring his accordion and Kit had been shaving
candles to wax the studio floor. She couldn't help
seeing, when they unpacked it almost right under
her nose, that the box from Boston was filled with
paper lanterns. Even collapsed they were pretty,
green and scarlet and gold. But she had pretended
not to notice. They wanted it all to be a lovely
surprise.

Presents, a picnic, a party! If only Mother were
here. . . .

A shadow dimmed, for a moment, the happy
prospects of the day. Mother had loved parties
and secrets and surprises. There was never anyone
like her for making happiness out of almost nothing

at all. "What do you think we're having for
supper?" she would ask in her singing voice, and
even if it was only baked apples it seemed like a
party with pink ice-cream just because Mother was
there.

Barbara felt a lump in her throat and her lashes
misted with tears. She hoped Mother knew they
were all together again in the gray-shingled Provincetown house, that Father hadn't married anybody as Aunt Josephine said he would, that Kit
wasn't as lame as he used to be, and Gay was a
beauty, and Jamie was a dear little boy with freckles
all over his face. Mother had loved them all so
much. She hoped that Mother knew. . . .

The house was coming to life. Downstairs in
the kitchen Martha was banging stove-lids and
noisily clattering pans. There were sounds over-
head in the attic where Kit had quarters of his own.
"Chips" was looking for Jamie and barking as loud
as he could. Barbara popped out of bed. She
couldn't wait for the happy day to begin. Besides,
it was safer to grab the bathroom before the children were up.

> *"We sail the ocean blue*
> *We catch-a da plenty-a fish"*—

she hummed as, fresh from a shower, she brushed
her soft brown hair. Perhaps she should "do it
up" now that she was eighteen. But the pins
wouldn't hold and the curly ends kept slipping out

of the knot. She tied a ribbon around her head and
let the shoulder-length mop swing free. Alice-in-
Wonderland. Again the gay little smile woke the
dimple that wanted to sleep.

Thinking of Bruce, she bent toward the mirror.
He said her face was the shape of a heart. It was,
she discovered with a feeling of pleased surprise.
And he said her eyes were like pansies, sometimes,
soft and velvety brown, but that, sometimes, they
turned into shining dark stars that did something
queer to his breath. The girl in the mirror flushed
and Barbara's cheeks felt warm. Silly! Bruce was
teasing, of course. He said the same sort of things
to Gay.

> *"We sail the ocean blue*
> *We catch-a da plenty-a fish"*—

This was one of her pretty days! Barbara's feet
did dance steps on the rug in front of the dresser.
She was never "a beauty" like Gay. Her nose
tilted up and her mouth was too wide. But, at least,
she was pretty to-day. Her cheeks were flushed and
her lips were red and her eyes were dark and shining. Only her skin was too fair to tan nicely, and
always, in the summer, there were freckles across
her nose. Bruce said —— Gracious!—Why
couldn't Bruce MacLain keep out of her private
thoughts? . . .

"Happy birthday, Bab!"

Barbara turned from the mirror. Gay stood in

the open doorway, poised like a butterfly about to light on a rose.

Gay was fourteen. She had bright brown curls foaming all over her head, and hazel eyes, with long curled lashes, and her skin was the tawny pink and gold of an apricot in the sun. She knew she was lovely, Barbara thought. There she was drifting toward the mirror, straight as a homing pigeon. But that was Aunt Lola's fault. . . .

"Aren't you excited?" Gay asked in her fluty voice.

"Terribly," Barbara answered. . . . What should she wear? Clothes for a picnic. Sandals and socks. The old brown skirt. Gracious! There was a dreadful rip in her favorite yellow jersey. . . .

"What do you suppose Uncle Stephen will send?" Gay, aping Barbara, was trying the effect of a ribbon around her curls.

"I can't even imagine." Barbara buckled her sandals, smiling because Gay called her godfather "Uncle Stephen" in that familiar sort of way. The children all called him "Uncle Stephen." The story of her christening never lost its charm. They liked Father to tell them about the village in southern France, the church with its bright-robed saints, the strange young American whom Father had invited to be her godfather. But he wasn't a "young" American now. He must be as old as Father. . . .

"Something nice, I suppose." Gay had discarded

the ribbon and was dabbing perfume behind her ears.
" Uncle Stephen sends lovely gifts."

" Beautiful," Barbara agreed, searching for a
needle and thread to mend the rip in her jersey. A
present every birthday. " Uncle Stephen " never
forgot the fifteenth of October. Sometimes the gift
was delayed because they had moved so often. But,
eventually, it caught up with them, its wrappings
smudged and torn and scrawled all over with forwarding addresses. He had remembered, too, that
babies grow into little girls and little girls grow up.
The gift, each year, was appropriate to the birthday. Where was the yellow thread? Everything
was helter-skelter this morning. . . .

" I wish I was eighteen."

" What would you do? " Barbara had found a
needle and thread. She sat, tailor fashion, on the
sea-chest beneath the window, mending the rip in
her jersey with long uneven stitches. " What would
you do, Gay Thorne, if you were eighteen years
old? "

" I'd marry somebody very rich," Gay answered
dreamily. " I'd have a squirrel coat and a limousine
and a bell to ring for the maid."

" You'd better learn to spell, first! "

That was Kit. Barbara glanced toward the door.
Kit was pulling on a sweater and his head, when it
popped through the sweater's neck, was a dark
tousled mop, darker than Gay's or her own, dark
like Father's and wavy, too. All the Thornes,

Barbara thought with a certain degree of complacence, had naturally curly hair.

Kit—Christopher for Father—was sixteen and tall for his age and, as Martha said, no amount of feeding would "put any meat on his bones." His eyes were hazel, like Gay's, and his lashes were almost as long. He hated it when ladies said, "What a sensitive face!" and he tried to make himself healthy and strong, exercising with dumb-bells, swimming, rowing a boat. He liked to study and the principal of the high school said he had "an extraordinary mind." He could draw, too, but he was shy and embarrassed about the things he did. Uncle Herbert's boys had teased him because he wanted to be an artist. . . .

"A child like you!" Kit frowned severely at Gay. "You'd better learn something before you talk about getting married. What do you think, Babs?—she spells stomach with a 'k'!"

"I guess that doesn't matter," Gay said airily. "I guess if I married somebody rich, I never would have to spell."

But she looked embarrassed, Barbara thought. She hated Kit to think she was less than perfect.

"Happy birthday, Babs!" Kit walked across to the chest and stood smiling at her, a flush in his thin dark cheeks, his hazel eyes very bright. "Lots of happy birthdays." He stooped and kissed her shyly, just touching the tip of her ear.

She couldn't answer just then. She looked down

at the needle which seemed suddenly to have blurred. Kit's limping walk brought a lump into her throat. He was the nicest one of them all. It wasn't fair that he should have to be lame. But certainly he was better. There had been two years, when he was a child, that Kit hadn't walked at all. . . .

" Did you do it? "

Barbara, puzzled, glanced up. But the question wasn't for her. Kit was looking at Gay. Gay nodded her head. Secrets, Barbara thought. Something about the party. . . .

" Stout fella' ! " Kit said.

Barbara saw Gay's warm color deepen. Kit's approval meant a very great deal to Gay.

It was wonderful, she thought when they had gone downstairs together, how Kit could manage Gay. Gay was spoiled. No wonder, with everybody telling her she was a beauty and the artists wanting to paint her and boys always hanging around the gate. And two years with Aunt Lola was enough to turn any child's head. But she worshipped Kit. If they weren't separated again until they were all grown up . . .

Until they were all grown up . . . Barbara looked out through the window, down over the roofs of the houses on Commercial Street, over the fish sheds and jutting wharves, across the harbor to the horizon where the water seemed to meet the sky in a dazzle of shining blue. She saw them all grown up, Kit and Gay and Jamie.

Kit would be a famous artist with paintings in all the exhibitions and the newspapers making a fuss. Gay probably would marry somebody very rich. She would come to visit in her squirrel coat with a limousine and a chauffeur and one small daughter as pretty and graceful as Gay. Jamie would be a naturalist, perhaps. His pockets were always stuffed with toads and star-fish and things.

And Barbara? She would stay in Provincetown with Father. She loved the gray-shingled house and the willow trees and the view across the harbor. Father could paint the things he liked when the children all were grown. Bruce would come in the summer and take her swimming and play his guitar for her and dance with her, evenings, at the " Ship." And maybe sometime . . .

Barbara bounced off the chest and pulled on the jersey with a jerk. "Silly!" she scolded herself. "When it comes to making up nonsense, you're exactly as bad as Gay!" But the scolding was not effective. It failed to cool her scorching cheeks or hush the birds in her heart.

Footsteps sounded on the stairs, Jamie's footsteps, sturdy and independent. Barbara met him in the hall. Jamie was clean, for a wonder,—but then it was early in the day. His hair was slicked down with water and all of his freckles shone. " Chips," the small yellow dog, was frisking wildly around his feet.

" Babs," Jamie said a bit breathlessly, " Martha

says for goodness sake will you please come down to breakfast before the muffins get cold."

Barbara kissed the messenger and gave him a hearty squeeze. But Jamie wriggled away. He was twelve years old and objected to being kissed. With his ears very red he plunged down the steps and " Chips " scampered behind.

They were waiting for her at the foot of the stairs, Father and Kit and Jamie and Gay. A chorus of " Happy Birthday!" rose to greet her, beautiful wishes with wings. Barbara smiled her gayest smile and her sandalled feet did skipping steps to a little tune of their own. Presents, a picnic, a party! Because she was happy and loved them so much, she sang as she danced down the stairs:

> " We sail the oecan blue
> We catch-a da plenty-a fish "—

Martha came out from the dining-room. Her face was the picture of woe.

" Sing before breakfast, you'll cry before night," she said in a warning voice.

That set them all to laughing. Martha's face was so droll!

II

Barbara sat with Father in the sun on the wide front steps. The children had gone to school. Mr.

Tubbs, the postman, had left the mail and gone whistling on his way. Martha had shooed her out of the kitchen and told her not to come back. As though she didn't know, by the smell, that Martha was making cake!

Lovely day! You'd think it was summer except that the willows were turning brown. The sunshine was warm and brilliant; the air was like golden wine. In the borders along the walk the petunias were still in bloom, disks of velvet, purple and lavender, claret red. Everything seemed washed in gold. October in Provincetown, Barbara thought, was the nicest month of the year.

"What time is it, Babbie?" Father asked.

She knew he was teasing. He asked every five minutes so she could consult the watch "Uncle Stephen" had sent. She had to admire it often, the delicate carving, the ribbon strap, the sapphire in the stem.

"Half-past ten," she answered and then, pleased and excited, her voice like a shaken chime of bells, "Isn't it beautiful, Father? How do you suppose Uncle Stephen knew I wanted a watch?"

"The man is a magician."

Father was smiling at her. She thought how handsome he was, his hazel eyes, his thick dark hair, his lean straight body that made him look so young. Kit looked like Father but Kit was more grave. He would never have Father's ringing laugh, his happy-go-lucky charm.

"What does Aunt Josephine say?" Father indicated the letter that lay in Barbara's lap.

"She told me to take care of my complexion as that was my one claim to beauty."

"What else?"

Barbara hesitated. There were, in the letter, many references to Father and none of them were flattering.

Father relieved her embarrassment.

"She said she hoped you weren't growing up like heathen"—his eyes twinkled wickedly—"though that, perhaps, was too much to expect since Christopher Thorne has no more idea how to bring up children than a crow in a corn field knows about running for Congress."

"It wasn't a crow in a corn field." Barbara dimpled and smiled.

"A cat on the back fence, then."

"How did you know?" Barbara asked, surprised.

"I am familiar with all of her similes." Father lit a cigarette. "Directly or indirectly, I've heard them many times."

Father leaned back against the wall of the house, the blue gray smoke curling in wreaths above his head. He seemed to be thinking amusing thoughts. Father made jokes about everything—even Aunt Josephine.

Barbara looked down at the letter. The writing on the envelope recalled the brick house in Providence, the elms and the urns on the lawn, Aunt

Josephine herself, majestic and awe-inspiring. She seemed to hear the yapping bark of Aunt Josephine's bad-tempered poodle, Cousin Evie's twittery voice agreeing with Aunt Josephine no matter what she said, the solemn important ticking of the grandfather's clock in the hall.

Aunt Josephine was Mother's aunt. Barbara had lived with her two years, the two years after Mother died when the children had been parcelled out among the relatives and Father had gone away. It wasn't a happy two years. Aunt Josephine didn't approve of artists. She didn't approve of Father. Barbara, remembering, sighed. She had missed the children so much. Night after night she had cried herself to sleep with her head buried under the pillow so Aunt Josephine wouldn't hear.

Three years of being together again hadn't made her forget. Sometimes, even now, she thought, for a dreadful moment, that they were separated. In the night, sometimes, the thought would come, so real, so frightening, that she would have to creep into Gay's room to see if Gay was there, into Father's room and Jamie's, up to Kit's quarters in the attic, before her heart would stop thumping and she could sleep again. . . .

"What are you thinking?" Father's voice, blessedly near, routed the dismal thoughts of those past times.

But she didn't tell him about them. It didn't seem quite polite. Father might think she didn't trust him. He had promised that they should never be " parcelled out " again.

" I was thinking," she answered instead, " that the harbor won't look the same when the *Ariel* isn't there."

They saw her swaying at anchor, her sails gleaming white in the sun, Mr. Loring's sloop, the *Ariel*, beautiful as a dream.

" Jim is leaving to-morrow." Father spoke regretfully. " He asked me to go for a farewell sail this afternoon."

" That will be nice."

Barbara was glad for Father. He loved sailing and boats. The ships he painted were the pictures people bought. " Tripe," Father called them. They weren't as nice as the things he did before Mother died. They were up in the attic collecting dust. People preferred the ships.

Father's attention strayed from the *Ariel*.

" Babbie," he asked, taking a letter from his pocket, " do you remember Mr. Schwartz? "

" That dreadful old man with the whiskers? "

" Be more respectful, young lady." Father pretended to be stern. " He was an angel in disguise."

" Why? " Barbara asked, thinking that old Mr. Schwartz looked less like an angel than anyone she had ever seen in her life. Were there gentlemen angels? She never could be quite sure.

" He's building a swanky home, a castle on the Rhine. No, not the Rhine "—Father consulted the letter—" the Hudson, to be exact, and he wants ship panels in his library and ——"

"Father! He wants you to paint them!"

"That's the reward for being polite to gentlemen with whiskers."

"Father!" Barbara was bouncing with excitement. "We can buy the rest of the house and put in a heater and mend the roof and ——" A gulp stemmed the torrent of words. The prospect of sudden riches had taken away her breath. "Father," she urged when she had found it again, "go send him a telegram right away."

"I'm going." He stretched his legs and stood up. "Don't open the studio door."

"Why not?" she asked, pretending not to know what he meant.

"Lions in there. They snap off pretty girls' heads."

Father swung down the walk and hurdled the picket fence. Barbara, watching, saw him turn down Pearl Street, bare-headed, the wind tossing his hair. How young he looked and healthy and brown. There was that silly Miss Mifflin stopping him at the corner. If she knew what Father thought of her chirping voice and her girlish airs . . .

Lovely day! Oh, everything was so nice! They could finish buying the house. Dear Mr. Schwartz! She loved even his whiskers. Aunt Josephine's letter couldn't bother her now. But it was a blot on the day. She would bury it out of sight.

She found a stick and scooped out a hole under the willow tree. That was the end of Aunt Josephine. She heaped up the earth and stuck in a twig for a headstone. A petunia for a wreath. It should have a ribbon with " Rest in Peace." But she was laughing and humming Bruce's song . . . " We sail the ocean blue " . . . She tried to compose her features and think of a dismal hymn . . .

" Hello, there—Happy Birthday! "

Barbara looked up from Aunt Josephine's premature grave. She felt her heart beat faster. Bruce was unlatching the gate.

III

The picnic basket was packed with lunch. The presents had been displayed: Father's coral necklace, Kit's water color of the willows, Gay's slipper buckles, the window box Jamie had made, filled with vines and blossoming plants. Bruce had admired them all. He had heard about old Mr. Schwartz who had turned out to be an angel in disguise. Of course there were gentlemen angels, he said. But he doubted if they wore whiskers.

Now he was in the kitchen talking secrets with Martha. Barbara had tactfully remained in the living-room. Waiting was difficult. She struck a few notes on the piano, drifted from the piano to the window box, from the window box to the door. Her feet, which would keep skipping, rumpled the soft rag rugs. She was too excited to lay them straight. Why didn't Bruce hurry? It was after eleven o'clock!

She looked at herself in the mirror above the book shelves set in its frame of tarnished gilt. The freckles *were* growing fainter, she thought. Milkweed Cream. "After three applications," the book of instructions had said. She would try it again to-night.

The kitchen door opened and there was Bruce. She saw him, his head above hers, framed in the oval of tarnished gilt. Bruce tanned a lovely color, she thought, sort of golden brown and his hair was golden brown, too, like beech leaves in the fall. His eyes were blue. That was always surprising. You expected them to be brown. They were smiling, crinkling at the corners . . .

"Do you like her?" Bruce asked.

"Do you?" She whirled around, bold as brass because it was her birthday.

"She's pretty nice." His eyes said more than that. Or maybe she just imagined it. You couldn't tell about Bruce . . .

"Are you ready?" He came into the room with the basket of lunch. Martha followed, flapping her apron at a fly.

"I've been waiting hours!" She didn't feel bold any longer. She felt sort of happy and shy.

"My heavenly stars!" Martha's voice sounded cross. She stood with her hands on her hips, a wiry wisp of a woman buttoned into a stiffly starched print frock. "What *have* you been doin', Babbie Thorne? The rugs are all rucked up!"

"My feet are excited," Barbara said. "I can't make them keep still."

"You never can!" Martha did her best to look very tall and severe. "I never saw such a flighty child in all the born days of my life!"

"It's her birthday, Martha," Bruce said gently. . . . Darling! he thought, watching Barbara. Darling! . . .

"Oh, Martha doesn't mean it!" Barbara caught her around the waist and waltzed her across the floor. "She has to sound important."

"Stop it! You stop it!" Martha gasped. "Dancin' at my age!" she sputtered when Barbara released her. "They'd have me put out of the church!"

"Got everything?" Bruce asked. . . . Alice-in-Wonderland. The ribbon around her hair. Was she thinking of him when she tied that perky bow? . . .

"Oh, the beach ball!"

"It's under the dinin'-room table"—Martha was shaking the rugs and placing them straight on the floor—"though if that's any place for a ——"

Barbara checked the words with a strangling hug. "Good-bye, Marthy-Ann," she said and left a kiss on Martha's cheek.

They went out through the dining-room door, under the arbor that led from the house to the studio, under the swaying willows.

" Babbie ——" Bruce stopped suddenly and set the basket on the grass.

Barbara stopped, too. She looked up at him wonderingly above the beach ball held against her chest in the circle of both of her arms. Shadows flickered across his hair, his face, his flannel shirt, sunlight, shadow, as the willow branches moved in the gentle wind. His eyes weren't smiling now. They looked at her so strangely . . .

" Did you think I hadn't brought you a present? " he asked.

" I didn't know."

" Would you have minded if I hadn't? " he said gravely.

" I couldn't have borne it," she answered.

" Shut your eyes and give me your hand."

The ball bounced down on the grass. Barbara screwed her eyes together and held out her small right hand. She knew the present was a ring before he said she might look. Such a lovely ring! It was made of twisted gold and from a tiny clasp in the center hung a small gold heart which made a tinkling sound whenever she moved her hand.

" Bruce! " She lifted her face, flushed and starry-eyed, framed in blowing tendrils of soft brown hair. A smile that was close to tears trembled across her lips. " Bruce! " she marvelled. " It just exactly fits! "

"It should," he said. "It was made for you. The heart is to match your face."

They were silent for an interval. The wind in the willows was a song that was happy and sad. Barbara moved her hand and heard the tinkling of the heart. She wanted to thank him. She couldn't find words. She looked down at the grass, afraid she was going to cry.

Bruce saw the droop of the curly head. What was she thinking? Did the ring mean more to her than a birthday gift?

"Babbie ——"

A low little laugh broke the spell of sunlight and shadow and the willows' sad sweet song. Barbara raised her head. Her face sparkled with mischief.

"Gracious!" she cried. "We're standing on top of Great-aunt Josephine's grave!"

CHAPTER II

I

THE car, a roadster with battered fenders and one blind headlight, rattled along Commercial Street, threatening at every jounce to shake itself into bits. Bruce had put the top down and the wind tousled Barbara's hair. She'd have a dreadful time to-night, combing out all the snarls. But she didn't mind. It was fun to feel the wind in her hair. It was fun to be riding with Bruce.

"Comfortable?" he asked, above the noise of the engine.

She nodded and then exclaimed, "Oh, Bruce! Just look at Miss Abbie's dahlias! Aren't they lovely! So big!"

The dahlias against the low white house were tufted rosettes of satin, yellow and amber, deep wine-red. Bruce gave them scant attention. He was looking, side-wise, at the small excited person whose shoulder brushed his arm. When he was alone he thought he knew her by heart, the way her hair waved back from her forehead, her tilted nose, the dimple that woke when she smiled. And yet, each time he saw her again, she was a fresh surprise. Darling! he thought, watching her wave a greeting to Jake Preble on his dray. Lovely child! . . .

"Bruce!" Her voice, laughing, a little startled, forced his eyes back to the narrow street. "Bruce!" She sighed with relief. "You missed it by half an inch!"

They left the town behind. The road stretched before them, curving, dipping in places, following the uneven line of the shore. Bruce gave the car the gas. Barbara liked to travel at top speed over this stretch of road. It was like a roller-coaster, she said. He heard her little excited squeals. He felt her hand clutch his arm. She enjoyed things so, little things, presents, the prospect of a party, swooping in a ramshackle Ford along a curving road. Life was an adventure to Babbie. It would be always, he thought. Good Lord! Was that waddling thing a goose! . . .

The car swerved with a sudden jolt and stopped on the brink of a ditch. Barbara tumbled against him. He felt her hair, silky and soft, brushing across his cheek. . . .

"Did we hit it?" she asked breathlessly.

"I don't think so." He found it difficult to keep his mind on the goose.

They looked back. The goose, safe at the side of the road, glared at them, scolded shrilly, smoothed its ruffled feathers.

" It looks like old Mrs. Jackson "—Barbara said
—" when she's fussing at Jamie and ' Chips.' "

She smiled up at him through a tangle of wind-
blown hair. She had looked like that, Bruce
thought, three summers ago, the day he first had
seen her. That day she had tumbled into his arms.
He had been coming out of her father's studio and
suddenly a small figure with bare legs and a mop of
curly brown hair had slid down the studio roof
straight into his arms.

" Aunt Josephine wouldn't let me slide down
things," she said, when she had recovered her voice.

" Aunt Ida wouldn't let me," he had answered.

After that they were friends. He had gone to
the gray-shingled house very often. Christopher
Thorne was an interesting man. And he had been
charmed by the little Thornes. The haphazard
household was a constant delight. But Barbara was
his favorite. Her changing moods bewildered and
amused him. She was like an April day, he thought,
all smiles and tears and tempers and unexpected
whims. During the months he was not in Provincetown, he thought of her. Lovely things brought her
into the foreground of his mind, a primrose, an early
star, a pair of tiny slippers. . . .

" Are we going to Long Nook, Bruce? " Barbara's voice recalled him from the past. " Or shall
we invite the goose and just have the picnic here? "

" I'm sorry." He smiled an apology and
promptly released the brake.

The car rattled on down the curving road. They passed low white houses and apple trees; the Truro church, square and white, its steeple pricking through tinted foliage; a windmill slowly turning; fence rails massed with goldenrod; swampy meadows where red and white cows drowsed in the autumn haze. Barbara chattered gayly, discovered wonders along the way. Bruce was silent, lost in thought.

What would she have said, he wondered, if he had put the ring on her other hand? He had wanted to but he had been afraid. She looked so young in that yellow jersey with the ribbon around her hair. Did she understand that he loved her, as a man loves a woman, that he wanted to share the adventure of her life? There were times when she seemed grown up. But this morning, under the willows, except for a moment, her eyes had been younger than Gay's. Better wait. But suppose he should lose her. Some-one would always be falling in love with Barbara. He was leaving to-morrow . . .

"This is the place to turn, Bruce, in case you hadn't noticed."

"I hadn't," he confessed, turning from the main road into the road that led, through a stretch of woods, to the ocean. "I'm absent-minded to-day."

Barbara, silent now, watched the trees running past. What was Bruce thinking? He was so quiet, looking straight ahead. Was he, too, feeling sad, in spite of being so happy? He seemed to have for-gotten her. She had only imagined that, under the willows, he had looked at her in a different sort of way. She felt, all at once, very small and lost and forlorn.

But the feeling vanished when they scrambled down the steep drop of slipping sand to the beach. She couldn't feel forlorn. It was such a beautiful day. Under his flannel shirt and old duck trousers Bruce wore his bathing suit. Barbara stripped off her sandals and socks and waded along the shore. Gracious, the water was cold! Her toes felt frozen. How could Bruce stand it to stay in so long?

They raced down the wide white beach until he was warm again. They played with the beach ball and invented a brand new game. It was fun to shout and sing and make a lot of noise. There was no one to hear them. They were alone in a world of sand and sunshine, a blue and golden world, sunshine and ocean and sky.

They opened the basket of lunch and gobbled like greedy children. Everything tasted so good, the sandwiches, the tarts, the coffee poured piping hot from the thermos bottle into the tin cups Bruce had brought. And there was a surprise in the bottom of the basket—maple candy stuffed with hickory nuts. Martha had bothered to make it. Wasn't Martha a dear?

When they couldn't hold another crumb, they stretched out on the blankets. Bruce lit a cigarette and blew smoke rings, one inside the other. Barbara admired them. She admired Bruce. He was

so good looking, his golden brown tan, his eyes that
were as deeply blue as the sky on a frosty night.
It was fun to be with him, lying there, drowsy and
warm, washed with waves of sunlight. Because she
was happy she hummed the song that all day long
had been singing through her mind—

" We sail the ocean blue
We catch-a da plenty-a fish "—

Bruce heard the low humming sound. He
propped himself on his elbow to see her more distinctly. She lay, curled like a kitten, her eyes half
closed, her head pillowed on her arm. Tenderness
swelled in his heart.

" Babbie," he said gently.

" Hmm? "

" Babbie . . . I'm leaving to-morrow. "

The humming ceased. Her brown eyes opened
wide.

" Leaving, Bruce? "

" Going back to New York."

Barbara turned her head. She didn't want Bruce
to see her face. She knew she was going to cry.

It was strange, she thought, that she should want
to cry about Bruce. Last year and the year before
he was just one of the young artists who came, in
the summer, to Provincetown and were always stopping in at the house to talk to Father and look at
his paintings and drink his wild cherry wine. Only
Bruce was nicer looking than any of the others,

more friendly and amusing. Father liked him especially. The children liked him, too. And she had
liked him—the way she liked old Ramon the shoe-
maker and Manuel who took her sailing and Jake
Pringle and Tommy Lynne and all of her Provincetown friends. . . .

" Babbie! Look at me, Babbie. . . ."

She couldn't look at him then. She looked, instead, at a puffy cloud sailing across the sky. This
summer it had been different. From the very first,
she decided. It was the way Bruce had looked at
her the day he came back to Provincetown last June.
She remembered the dress she wore, a bodice dress
with a long full skirt, the pale soft yellow of a primrose, and her hair had been pinned at the nape of her
neck just to try the effect. " You're growing up,
Babbie," Bruce had said and somehow the look in
his smiling blue eyes had made her feel happy and
shy. . . .

" Babbie, dear . . ."

His voice sounded sorry about something. Maybe
Bruce had guessed and was sorry because she loved
him so much. Her heart turned over with the surprise of a discovery. Why, she loved Bruce, not as
she loved Father and the children, but in another
way, the way Mother had loved Father. That was
why it had been different this summer. That was
why she wanted to cry, sometimes, and was always
imagining things. Bruce had guessed. He must
have known it all along, when he was teasing her

and telling her things about her eyes. Bruce had guessed. He was sorry because she loved him so much. . . .

"Babbie," he said again. "I'm leaving to-morrow. I'm going back to New York."

She felt so miserable she wanted to die. But Bruce mustn't be sorry for her. She swallowed past a sudden lump in her throat and made her voice sound gay.

"Well," she said, not looking at him, "I hope you'll have a nice trip."

Bruce heard her voice, gay and lilting and unconcerned. A shadow slipped across his face. He couldn't see that her lashes were wet with tears.

II

The sky had clouded over. Puffy white clouds, at first, and then, from the east, darker clouds, purple and black, moving faster and faster, blotting out the clear shining blue of the sky. The wind was rising.

"It's going to storm," Bruce said. "We'd better turn back."

They had walked a long way up the beach, quiet most of the time, both of them unhappy, thinking of things to say. The storm was a welcome diversion. It lifted them out of themselves. Their spirits rose with the rising wind. They were excited, glowingly alive.

"Where did it come from?" Barbara asked. "It's been a beautiful day."

"There was a red sky this morning." They had turned and were walking rapidly. The wind rose higher, blowing the sand, frothing the waves with white-caps. Far down the beach they saw, tiny specks in the distance, the basket, the heap of blankets, the beach ball no larger than a bead.

> *"Red sky at morning*
> *Sailors take warning,"*

Barbara sang, exhilarated by the wind. "That isn't good poetry, is it, Bruce?"

"Better save your breath," he advised.

He took her hand and they tried to run. The wind pushed them back. It was like a wall, moving against them, pushing them back. The blowing sand stung their eyes. The waves made a crashing sound, pounding against the shore.

"Bruce!" Barbara cried, clinging fast to his hand. "I can't move! I can't keep my feet on the ground!"

"Try," he shouted, bending his head so she could hear. "If we can make that shack ——"

They had noticed it as they walked up the beach, a shack made of planks and branches crazily nailed together, set in a sheltered curve of the sand bank. Children had built it, they thought; boys playing "Robinson Crusoe." They had smiled at it as they walked up the beach. Now it seemed a safe haven, a refuge from the storm. They made it after a struggle, dropped, breathless and panting, on the sand beneath the flimsy roof of pine branches.

It was a refuge of sorts. The sand no longer stung their eyes. In the sheltered curve of the sand bank they were protected from the fury of the wind. They crouched back against the sand bank grateful for shelter in a whirling purple-gray world. The small shack had no front wall. Through a film of blowing sand they saw the waves dashing up on the beach. They waited for the rain.

"No rain?" Barbara asked, after an interval of watching the waves through the blowing sand.

"It's a wind storm," Bruce answered. "Are you cold?"

"Sort of."

"Wish we had the blankets. Come here. There! That's better, isn't it?"

It was lovely, she thought, to have Bruce hold her close, to feel through the soft flannel shirt the comforting warmth of his body. The wind shook the flimsy roof. Pine needles fell upon them in sudden rust-brown showers. A screaming gull flew low along the shore-line. The waves were like white-maned horses galloping in a race. There was no rain.

"It's like the storm Manuel tells about." Barbara's voice was tinged with awe. "You remember, Bruce—when seventeen men were drowned. That storm came on a beautiful day."

Thinking of Manuel's story made her suddenly afraid. Why? She didn't know. It was like something seen through a fog, a dim white ghost of fear. A moment ago she had felt safe and warm. Now the wind frightened her. She shivered and pressed closer to Bruce.

"Frightened?" he asked, conscious of the shiver, conscious of the slight weight of her body, of the fragrance of her hair.

She nodded, seeing it still, the dim white ghost of fear.

"Why?"

"I don't know." She looked up at him, her eyes wide and startled. "I feel like Martha must when she says 'A goose walked over my grave.'"

"You're thinking of the goose in the road." His smile reassured her.

"Maybe." She laughed shakily. "Sing to me, Bruce."

"I'll tell you a story instead."

"That will be nice." She nestled against him, sighed. "A happy story, please."

Child, Bruce thought, feeling still the hurt of her unconcern, "I hope you'll have a nice trip." He saw her fingers curling around his hand and all other emotions were lost in tenderness. She was a frightened child, clinging to him, wanting to be comforted. . . .

"Once upon a time," he began, his lips close to her ear, "there was a gypsy boy who loved very

dearly a little gypsy girl. Her face was the shape
of a heart. The boy thought it was a beautiful face.
He saw it everywhere, in the clouds, in the forest
pools, in the flames of the gypsy fire. . . ."

Barbara, listening, almost held her breath. Was
it only a story? She forgot the storm, forgot to be
frightened. Was Bruce talking to her?

" They played in the woodland together," he continued, " the gypsy boy and the gypsy girl whose
face was the shape of a heart. The boy brought her
wild roses to wear in her hair and sandals for her
pretty feet and a ring of twisted gold. But he didn't
dare to tell her he loved her because she was a little
girl, no higher than his heart, and he wasn't sure
that she knew about being in love. . . ."

Barbara's heart beat fast. A ring of twisted
gold! She pressed it against her cheek.

" The boy had a silver flute," Bruce continued.
" He played it only for her. At night when the
moon was shining he played for her on his silver
flute. The flute knew only one song—' I love you,
little gypsy girl with the roses in your hair.' He
hoped she would understand the song of the silver
flute. He hoped she would love him, too. . . ."

She heard it singing in her heart, the song of the
silver flute. It was amazing but it was true.
Through the roar of the wind she heard silver
notes, sprinkling showers of silver notes, high and
sweet and clear. Barbara lifted her head, saw the
expression in Bruce's eyes, saw and understood.

The smile that was close to tears touched her lips again.

"She understands," she said softly. "She knows about being in love."

III

The storm had blown itself out. They saw traces of it as, very much later, they drove slowly back toward town. The road was strewn, in places, with branches and broken limbs. The goldenrod was flattened against the ground. A maple tree which, that morning, had flaunted its crimson and gold, stood naked and shivering in drifts of ragged leaves.

The wind was quiet, now, and sunset colors, deepening into night, streaked the sky in the West. The harbor grew calm and the stars came out and the red eye of the lighthouse beacon winked from the end of the breakwater as though this had been an ordinary day. The storm was no longer a menace. It was something to talk about when men sat in stores on winter evenings and ladies met to make aprons for the Methodist Christmas bazaar.

"Happy?" Bruce asked, above the noise of the engine.

"Mmm!" Barbara nestled closer into the curve of his arm. It wasn't all being happy, she thought. There was sadness in it, too,—like hearing beautiful music or lighting the candles on Christmas Eve. She felt different, older, quite grown up. It didn't seem possible that only this morning she had been perfectly happy because it was her birthday and there were going to be presents and a party.

"Bruce," she said, thinking aloud.

"Hmm?"

"I'll never be perfectly happy again."

"Why not?" he asked, surprised and a little hurt.

"Because," she gravely explained, "I'll always be thinking about all the taxis that could run over you and germs and bombs and things."

"Darling!" The anxiety in her voice amused and touched him. "Go with me to-morrow," he said softly. "Don't let's wait."

"I couldn't, Bruce," she said firmly, although her heart beat faster at the thought. "If we put in a heater, I'll have to be here because anybody could cheat Father. And I'll have to see Miss Abbie about making some dresses for Gay and Jamie ought to have his tonsils out and ——"

"Fall house cleaning, I suppose," he teased, "and beach plum jelly and the winter flannels to hang on the line and air."

"Don't tease, Bruce." Her hand on his arm asked him to understand. "You know how Father is. He's a darling but he just doesn't know about dresses and tonsils and things. I ——" Her voice trembled. "I don't know how they'll manage ——"

Bruce heard a stifled sob. His arm tightened around her.

"They'll manage," he said. "Martha is efficient. And you'll be here in the summer. Perhaps in a year or two we can give up the job in New York. . . . At Christmas, Babbie "—his lips were against her hair—" if you won't go with me to-morrow? "

"Yes," she promised gravely. "If Father doesn't mind."

"Darling! I love you so much."

There were lights in the gray-shingled house. Together they unlatched the gate and walked up the path to the steps.

"What will your father say?" Bruce asked, holding tight to her hand.

"Father loved Mother very much," she answered softly. "I think he will understand."

She stood on the lowest step and the light from the fanlight fell on her curly brown hair. Bruce saw, in the deepening dusk, her shining dark eyes, the grave little smile that curved her soft red lips.

"Babbie," he asked, "do you hear it now—the song of the silver flute? "

"I'll always hear it," she said.

"Always? "

"Forever and ever."

"Darling, darling! I love you so much."

The front door opened and Kit stood in the bright rectangle of light.

"Is that you, Babs?" His voice sounded strained and hoarse.

"What is it?" she asked, her heart thumping wildly with fright.

"I—we——" Kit paused and gulped. Barbara knew he was trying not to cry.

"What is it?" she asked again, impatiently shaking his arm.

"It—it's Father," Kit answered, not trying, now, to choke back unmanly tears. "He went sailing with Mr. Loring and the wind broke the rigging and the boom must have hit Father because when they got him——"

"Father!" The word was a heart-broken sob. All of the color ebbed out of her cheeks. Her eyes were tragically large. "Oh no, Kit! No!"

Tears splashed over Kit's thin cheeks. His chin quivered like a child's.

"Babs!" he sobbed. "Father's drowned!"

CHAPTER III

I

PEOPLE were kind. All day they came to the gray-shingled house. Mrs. Loring left Mr. Loring, who was threatened with pneumonia, to ask if there wasn't *something* she could do. Father's artist friends came to ask the same kind question. Miss Abbie brought all of her precious dahlias which had survived the storm. Miss Harlowe sighed over the " poor dear kiddies " and wept into a handkerchief scented with mignonette. Manuel and his friends left so many offerings of fish that Martha was distracted. Everybody was sorry and kind and anxious to help.

Cousin Evie arrived from Providence and was installed in Gay's room. Aunt Josephine, she reported, was just getting over " one of her spells " and would come as soon as the doctor gave her permission to travel. Cousin Evie was tall and thin with crimped yellow-gray hair and a long pink nose. In Providence she was merely Aunt Josephine's echo, a " poor relation," often enough snubbed and disregarded. In the gray-shingled house she felt important. She hoped people would notice how helpful she was, how gentle with the children.

Cousin Julia came from Augusta, Maine, and Jamie moved up with Kit. Cousin Julia felt important wherever she was because she was Aunt Josephine's daughter. She was large and rosy and handsome and very efficient and kind. When the little Thornes had been " parcelled out," she had taken Jamie. She supposed she would take him again, though she would rather have had Barbara or Gay. Boys tracked in so much dirt. She thought of her new Wilton rugs and sighed and asked Martha for a broom.

Aunt Lola wired from Florida where she had gone for the winter. She was leaving at once, the telegram said. She sent them all a great deal of love, especially " dear little Gay." Uncle Herbert wired from his office in Pittsburgh that business would detain him there until the end of the week. After that, he would start for Provincetown. He and Aunt Emma and the boys sent sympathy and love. If they needed money, as they probably did, they were to wire collect.

The Thornes clung to each other, dazed, bewildered, shaken with grief. The house no longer seemed their own, a pleasant friendly place. It was, all at once, so painfully tidy and neat. They were more comfortable out of doors. There, at least, everything was as it had always been; the willow,

trees, the grass still green in the warmth of Indian
summer, the small bronze dahlias growing along
the fence.

They sat together on the studio steps, Gay pressing close to Kit, Jamie's head against Barbara's
knee, " Chips " stretched out in the sunshine across
their feet. Sometimes they talked about Father,
remembering little things; a happy day in the dunes,
a bird-house he had built for them, a song he used
to sing. Sometimes they were silent and each knew
what the others were thinking though no one put
it into words. They were to be separated again—
this time, perhaps, forever.

The thought was never far from Barbara's mind.
She grieved for Father deeply and sincerely, but the
thought that the children might be separated was,
somehow, harder to bear. There were times when
she hoped that it needn't happen. Lying awake in
the low carved bed, with Gay asleep beside her, she
made elaborate plans. She would sell Father's
paintings, the lovely ones in the attic. She would
start a shop in the studio, hooked rugs and china
and etchings. She would take boarders in the summer. Somehow she would manage to keep the children together.

The plans seemed possible at night, lying awake
with Gay close and warm beside her. She would
see them living on in the gray-shingled house, a
shop in the studio, money to pay the bills. And,
sometime, Bruce would live with them here. Darling

Bruce! That would be such a nice arrangement. Sensible, too. Thinking of it, she would feel warm and safe and drowsy. Presently, she would tell herself a story. . . . "Once upon a time there was a gypsy boy who loved very dearly a little gypsy girl." . . . Before the story was finished, she would be fast asleep.

In the morning, however, with Cousin Julia managing everything and Cousin Evie acting as though she were no older than Gay, the plans would seem silly and childish. Bit by bit hope would vanish and her heart would feel heavy as lead. She seemed, visibly, to grow thinner. The color left her cheeks and her eyes were tragically large. "Now, Barbara," Cousin Julia would say, trying to be patient, "you'll be ill if you don't eat your supper." The words had no effect. Cousin Julia might as well have talked to the clock on the fireplace mantel.

Bruce, who had postponed his return to New York, was constantly at the Thornes'. But he seldom saw Barbara alone. She seemed content, in a measure, only when she was with the children. Loving her, it hurt him to know how completely they filled her mind. Occasionally he persuaded her to ride with him or to walk in the woods behind the town. But, though she went with him, as docilely as an obedient child, she was always anxious to return. Even when he held her in his arms, he felt that she wasn't there. Something had gone. The warm loving part of her which, for a few hours had been

his, was now absorbed by the children. He felt hurt
and helpless and left behind.

In his studio on one of the West End wharves,
Bruce spent many sleepless hours. Was she old
enough? he asked himself. Did she know how
deeply he loved her? Had he let himself in for
unhappiness? He asked her none of these questions. Loving her deeply, he tried, when he was
with her, to forget, for the moment, his own disturbing emotions. He knew she was glad that he
had postponed his return to New York. She would
drink the milk Cousin Julia prescribed if he held
the glass. When he left her at bedtime, she clung
to him. He found what comfort he could in small
inadequate things.

The gray-shingled house filled with flowers.
There were all sorts of letters and cards. Mr.
Tubbs, the postman, brought a stack of them twice
a day. He brought a letter from " Uncle Stephen."
It was a very nice letter. Barbara read it to the
children as they sat on the studio steps. " Uncle
Stephen " had seen in a paper, the letter said, an
account of Father's death. He sent sympathy to
his " little fillette."

" What's a ' fillette' ? " Gay wanted to know.

" That's French for goddaughter," Barbara explained.

" Is he a Frenchman? " asked Jamie, to whom
Frenchman meant the French-Canadians who lived
in Augusta, Maine.

"Of course not," Kit answered. "Don't you remember how Father used to tell us that he was the only other American, besides Mother and Father, in the town where Babs was born?"

"He must have been surprised." The story of Barbara's christening held a special charm for Gay. "Uncle Stephen must have been surprised to have Father ask him to be Babs' godfather when he didn't know him at all."

"He was probably pleased," Kit said proudly. "Everybody liked Father. Except"—he amended —"stuffy relations and people like that."

The children talked, in low voices, about Father. Barbara read the letter again. It was nice and friendly, she thought. She lingered over the concluding sentence . . . "If a crusty old bachelor can be of assistance, please let him know at once." . . . A crusty old bachelor! Then he wasn't married. And he must be older than she had thought. But he didn't sound "crusty." "Fillette" was a charming word. Saying it over made her feel that she knew "Uncle Stephen." . . . "My little fillette." . . . She tucked the letter inside her blouse and felt she had found a friend.

And then, on a day so blue and golden, so filled with sunshine and gentle wind and the smoky fragrance of autumn that it didn't seem possible there could be sadness in the world, they left Father beside Mother in the cemetery on the hill. The house seemed desolate when they returned, too quiet, too tidy and neat. Father was gone. Nothing was left of his songs and jokes, of his happy-go-lucky charm, nothing except his dusty paintings in the attic, his brushes and pipes in the studio, his memory in the loving hearts of the four sad little Thornes.

That evening they sat around the living-room hearth. It grew chilly when the sun went down and Bruce had built a fire. Cousin Evie had gone to bed with a headache. Cousin Julia, in Jamie's room upstairs, was writing a letter to Cousin Will. The children were glad to be alone. The room seemed more like home with the davenport drawn up to the hearth and Jamie lying with " Chips " on the rug in front of the fire. Barbara told them about the plans she made at night, lying awake in the low carved bed. The children accepted them with enthusiasm.

" I can get a job for after school," Kit said, his face brighter than it had been since the day of the storm. " In the *Advocate* office or somewhere. I'm sure I can get a job."

" Dicky Woods says I can be his delivery boy," Jamie announced from the hearth rug. " I've already asked him about it."

" If Martha goes, I'll do the dishes," Gay said nestling close to Kit, her head against his shoulder. " Even at breakfast," she promised.

" Stout fella' ! " Kit said softly, knowing how Gay hated washing dishes and dusting and making beds.

" Other people have shops," Barbara continued,

loving the children for wanting to help. She lifted her face to Bruce, feeling hopeful, wanting to be assured. "We could, couldn't we, Bruce? Isn't it a sensible plan? Don't you think we could?"

Bruce smiled but his eyes were grave. What a child she was, no older than Gay, making her fairy-tale plans. If he could bear it for her—the certain disappointment. She was too small to bear it herself, too young in spite of her courage. If he could bear it for her—he loved her, he loved her so much. . . .

The plans seemed possible, talking about them in front of the fire, surrounded by things that were familiar and friendly and dear. Barbara saw the shop in the studio, the rugs and etchings and china, Father's paintings against the walls, herself in a bodiced print frock talking to customers, smilingly making change. The children saw it, too. She could tell by their lighted faces, the look of relief in their eyes. They needn't be separated. They could stay in the gray-shingled house.

And then she knew that they couldn't. The plans vanished like bubbles touched by a careless hand. Cousin Julia, rosy and handsome and very kind, appeared at the living-room door.

"Ten o'clock," she said in the brisk cheerful voice that made Barbara feel small and rather foolish. "Time for tired kiddies to be in bed."

Kiddies! Was there ever in all the world such a hateful insulting word!

II

"We can't, can we, Bruce?" Barbara asked when the children, marshalled by Cousin Julia, had gone upstairs to bed. "We can't stay here together."

"I'm afraid not, Babbie," he answered, his face very troubled and grave.

"I guess I knew it all along," she said wearily. "Fairy tales." Her voice quivered. Looking down, he saw that her lashes were jewelled with tears.

"Don't mind so terribly, darling." He drew her into his arms, felt her trembling there, her hair against his cheek. "Please try not to mind so much."

"I—I can't help it, Bruce."

He knew that she couldn't help it. He knew that words were useless. He held her close, wanting to bear it for her, racked by her shaking sobs. Gradually the sobs grew less. She sighed and then was still, so still that he thought she had gone to sleep. But presently she stirred.

"Bruce. . . ."

"Yes, darling?"

"When are you going back to New York?"

"To-morrow. . . ."

She clung to him for a moment, then raised her head from his shoulder.

"I don't suppose ——" She paused and he saw, in the firelight, a faint pink flush creeping into her cheeks.

"What, Babbie?"

"I don't suppose ——" Her eyes were suddenly shy. "You couldn't take us with you—Kit and Gay and Jamie and me?"

"Why, Babbie ——"

"No, I suppose you couldn't." She was grown up, now, and reasonable, too reasonable for her years. "Shoes and things are expensive and boys eat such a lot."

"But I can take you." Bruce brushed the soft hair back from her brow. "You and I in my studio. We can count the stars through our skylight and every morning, for breakfast, I'll sing you a brand-new song."

Her eyes brightened. A little smile touched her lips.

"Bruce!" she whispered. "A new one every day!"

"And a special one for Sunday," he promised, loving the shine in her eyes.

It faded away, leaving her forlorn.

"You mustn't, Bruce."

"Wouldn't you like it?"

She nodded.

"Then why?"

"I have to think of the children." She squared her shoulders and lifted her firm little chin. "I'm the oldest. They've no one at all but me."

"They'll be cared for, darling," Bruce said huskily, thinking of her in his studio, seeing her curled like a kitten in his favorite easy chair. "You can't manage it, Babbie. Come with me to-morrow. I want you, I love you so much."

She drew away from him. Her eyes were hurt and unhappy.

"Bruce!" she said reproachfully. "I thought you would understand."

He knew he had blundered. He hastened to reassure her.

"I do understand," he said gravely. "I know how you'll all miss each other. But, darling ——"

"Kit hates it at Uncle Herbert's." She steadied the quivering of her lips. "They tease him because he wants to be an artist. Uncle Herbert will probably make him sell life insurance or something he wouldn't like. And Kit's so splendid, Bruce. Don't you see?"

Her hands crept up to his coat lapels, asked him to understand. "I can't bear it for Kit."

"I know." He kissed the pucker between her brows and felt a weight in his heart.

"And Aunt Lola is so silly," she continued, the words tumbling over each other in her eagerness to make Bruce understand. "She lives mostly in hotels since Uncle George died. That isn't good for a child like Gay. You should have seen her, Bruce; heels on her slippers and polished nails and her head full of silly notions. We almost couldn't stand her. She's different now. She worships Kit. And Jamie ——" She paused and drew a long breath.

"Don't, Babbie," Bruce said gently. "You're so tired. Don't think about it to-night."

"I can't help thinking. You've seen it, Bruce, the way Jamie looks at 'Chips.' Cousin Julia won't have a dog in the house. She's kind, of course, but she doesn't know about boys. And Jamie's so funny and dear."

"But what can you do?"

"Something," she said firmly.

"What, Babbie? Be sensible, dear."

"Something . . . I don't know."

Bruce felt a vague sort of fear. She looked so small and determined, so very dear in her velveteen frock with its childish white collar and cuffs. If he should lose her—"A bird nestles in your hand, yours to keep for always. Open your hand and the bird is lost in the sky." Where had he read that? Somewhere. . . .

"Babbie"—he held her closer, afraid she might slip away—"if you can't manage it, you'll come to me?"

"Yes, Bruce—if I can't."

He wanted to be further assured. Very gently he changed the birthday ring from her right hand to her left. The heart that matched her face made a tiny tinkling sound.

"Now we're engaged," he said.

"Yes," she sighed contentedly. "Now we're really engaged."

They were silent for a moment. A log in the

fireplace broke with a gentle cracking sound.
" Chips " on the hearth rug sighed and thumped his
tail.

" Babbie . . ."

" Hmm? "

" Do you love me? "

" Yes. . . ."

" Really, I mean? "

" Oh yes, Bruce—why? "

" I've wondered. . . .   You aren't very old."

" I am—inside," she said gravely. " You grow
up younger, Bruce, when you're the oldest and so
many things happen to you."

" Perhaps. . . .   Aren't you sleepy? "

" Yes. . . ."

" Want to go to bed? "

" I want to stay here with you."

" Darling. . . ."

" Tell me the story."

" Once upon a time there was a gypsy boy who
loved very dearly a little gypsy girl. . . ."

" Very dearly, Bruce? "

" More than anything in the world."

Quiet, now, weary, so weary, she lay against his
heart.

". . . The boy had a silver flute." . . .
Bruce softened his voice. She was going to sleep.
Poor tired baby! Her silky lashes drooped. The
hand which wore his ring crept slowly up to rest
against her cheek. . . . " The flute knew only

one song—'I love you, pretty gypsy girl with the roses in your hair. . . .'"

"Do you hear it, Babbie"—he asked gently—"the song of the silver flute?"

He thought that she did. She slept with a smile on her lips.

CHAPTER IV

I

THE house was full of relations. Aunt Lola's car stood at the gate, a beautiful car, dove-gray with silver fittings and a chauffeur named Pierre. Aunt Lola, small and plump, with massaged-looking skin and hair a shade too golden, sat beside the living-room fire wrapped in moleskin as soft as velvet. The weather had turned chilly and the stoves were not set up. Aunt Lola seldom left the chair beside the hearth. She pulled the moleskin closer when somebody opened a door and kept Martha busy making hot chocolate with quantities of whipped cream.

Gay was bewitched by Aunt Lola, her clothes, her jewels, the dove-gray car, the chauffeur named Pierre. Already she was different, Barbara thought, watching Gay adopt Aunt Lola's mannerisms, her gestures, the affected tones of her voice. She didn't want Gay to grow up into a silly little peacock, like Gwen, Aunt Lola's daughter, married now and, according to family gossip, " leading her husband a life." Mother would have hated it so. And Father, too. Gay could be so nice.

Uncle Herbert came and went, attending to business matters, interviewing the real estate agent and the officials at the bank. Uncle Herbert was not above medium height, ruddy and stockily built. But you felt that he was very tall and imposing. That, Barbara decided, was because of his pompous manner and the way he had of making small things seem important. Uncle Herbert "suffered from delusions of grandeur," Father used to say.

Uncle Herbert was kind to the children. He was especially kind to Kit.

"Well, Michael Angelo," he would say, " have you painted a masterpiece yet?"

He would laugh in a jolly way, meaning to be friendly. But Barbara, watching, would see Kit flush with embarrassment.

Or, pinching Kit's arm, he would say:

"No muscle!" He would pretend to be terribly shocked. "See here, young fellow, that won't do. Wait 'til we get you out in Pittsburgh. Roast beef is what you need."

Did he think they hadn't been properly fed? Barbara would try to choke back her indignation, knowing that Uncle Herbert meant only to be kind.

"You ought to see my young bruisers," Uncle Herbert would continue. "Hard as nails and strong as grizzlies. They'll give you a run for your money."

He would talk about Paul who played on his college football team and Joe who was a prep school star and Junior who had six medals for swimming although he was only fifteen. Barbara, an ache in her heart, would see Kit's flush deepen and a frightened look creep into his eyes. Kit couldn't play football. He would never be very strong.

Her last hope had vanished. She had pinned up her hair and worn her longest frock, but she knew that she looked as young and frightened as she felt, when she asked them to let her keep the children there in the gray-shingled house.

"Gracious!" Cousin Julia exclaimed. "What an absurd idea!"

"We could manage." Barbara felt her courage slipping away with the pins that held her hair. "You can live so cheaply in Provincetown. If Kit gets a job and we don't have Martha and——"

"It isn't only a question of money," Uncle Herbert said not unkindly. "There are many things to be considered. You're too young to assume such a responsibility. Besides," he added, "it isn't necessary."

It was necessary. She knew, in her heart, that it was necessary to keep the children together. But she couldn't put it into words. They confused her with grown-up logic. She shut herself up in the studio and cried helplessly with her cheek against Father's coat.

Aunt Josephine had decided not to come. The

change in the weather, she wrote, made the journey too great a risk, since she wasn't as young as she used to be and the Provincetown house had no proper sort of heat.   Barbara was to come to Providence with Cousin Evie.   She enclosed a generous check.

Barbara looked thoughtfully at the strip of pink paper signed in spidery writing with Great-aunt Josephine's name.   The check would take her to New York and buy her a winter coat.   A dress, perhaps.   Her wedding dress.   Aunt Josephine would make a fuss about Bruce.   She didn't approve of artists.   But Mother had married Father.

It would be lovely to be with Bruce, she thought, curled in a corner of the davenport, watching the lights in the fire.   She wouldn't mind if they hadn't much money.   She saw herself in his studio, sewing curtains while he painted, pouring his coffee at breakfast, having things warm and comfortable when he came home from the art school where he taught.

Darling Bruce!   She twisted his ring on her finger and heard the tinkling of the small gold heart. She hadn't told anybody.   The children thought it was a birthday ring.   The relations might make fun. She couldn't bear that.   Darling Bruce!   If it weren't for the children   . . .

The house was to be sold. Uncle Herbert decided that was best.   They couldn't understand why Barbara minded so much.

"Why should you want to keep it?" Cousin Julia asked in amazement.

"We like it, Cousin Julia." Never had the long low room seemed so charming and friendly and dear. Each piece of furniture was suddenly precious, the old square piano, Father's book shelves, the rugs Mother had dyed such lovely shades of russet and amber and brown. It was the only home they had known.

"No heating plant," Cousin Julia, brisk and efficient, enumerated the defects of the house. "No decent floors. The plumbing leaks and all the windows rattle. You'll be very lucky if anyone buys it."

Barbara hoped no one would. But she knew it was useless to explain. They never could understand. Her eyes brimmed over with tears.

"You're taking this much too hard," Cousin Julia said, trying to be patient. Uncle Herbert agreed. Cousin Evie quoted verses which had to do with " silver linings " and " sunrise after the storm." Aunt Lola gave her a turquoise ring. They humored her as though she were a rather bad-tempered child. She resented it fiercely. But she knew it was useless to talk. They never would understand.

Cousin Julia, assisted by Martha, thoroughly cleaned the house. Cousin Evie, excited and important, poked into closets and bureau drawers, wore smudges of dust on her long pink nose. Things were burned in the fireplace. There was little worth keeping, Cousin Julia said. Martha was to have the flower-box. Barbara packed her sea-chest with treasured odds and ends. She would have Martha send it to her in New York, the chest, the books, the low carved bed that Father had made. Everything else would be sold.

Their last day together arrived, a rainy day, chilly and depressing. The children's clothes were packed, untidy bundles of childish treasures, Father's painting, Mother's thin silver spoons. Martha's eyes were rimmed with red and her scolding voice was gentle. People from the town came to say good-bye.

"We'll miss you," they said. "The house won't seem the same."

Never the same again! Barbara, talking to Miss Abbie, realized it, all at once, with a sickening lurch of her heart. The house would belong to somebody else, the house that Mother had loved. They wouldn't see the willows grow green, next spring, and the apple tree burst into bloom. They wouldn't sit on the studio steps with "Chips" stretched out in the sunshine across their feet. . . .

Miss Abbie splintered into crystals, her apple cheeks, her glasses, the brooch that pinned her collar. Barbara ran blindly from the room, up the stairs, along the hall, up into the attic.

She heard a sound of sobbing. Kit lay on a broken sofa in the unused part of the attic, his face buried in his arms.

"Kit!" she cried softly, running to him, kneeling beside the sofa.

He raised a tear-stained face. His cheeks were hot and flushed. A feverish light burned in his hazel eyes.

"Sorry, Babs," he gulped, ashamed of crying, trying to be manly. "I didn't mean you to know about it."

"Do you mind so much about going with Uncle Herbert?" she asked, her heart breaking for Kit.

"I'd rather die," he said stormily. "I'd run away if I could. But I guess I wouldn't get far— with one leg that's not much good. Babs!" he was sobbing again, "why did it have to happen? Why can't we stay here together? Why did Father have to die?"

She couldn't answer his questions. There was nothing she could say. She held his head against her breast, fiercely maternal, wanting to bear it for Kit.

"You don't know what it's like, Babs," he sobbed, no longer ashamed. "Uncle Herbert's boys are so strong. I—I couldn't keep up. They laugh at things I say. They—they think I'm sort of crazy, I'd rather die than go back there."

It was dreadful to hear him sob. Kit so seldom cried; not even when he was a little boy and had to sit in a chair. He had always been shy and thoughtful and sensitive. He minded things so terribly. Those great boobies of Uncle Herbert's, Barbara thought. It wasn't fair. She must do something. Kit shouldn't suffer so.

"You needn't go with Uncle Herbert," she said, not very sure about anything, wanting only to hush his strangling sobs. "We'll all stay together, Kit."

He raised his head, a question in his eyes.

"We'll all run away together!" A plan presented itself to Barbara. She didn't know why she thought of it. Perhaps all along it had been lurking somewhere in the back of her mind. Perhaps it was a "presentment" like Martha had sometimes. Perhaps it was the ticking of the birthday watch on her wrist. "I know exactly what we'll do." Her voice sounded frightened, but happy, too. She felt her heart thumping against her ribs.

"What?" Kit asked hoarsely.

"We'll ——"

"Yoo-hoo!"

That was Cousin Evie coming up the steps.

"Shh!" Barbara whispered, her eyes dark with excitement, a warm pink flush in her cheeks. "In the studio after supper. I'll tell you about it then."

She pressed Kit's hand and felt his answering squeeze. He seemed happier already. Barbara lifted her chin and made a firm resolve. She'd do it no matter what happened. She must keep the children together.

Cousin Evie, wrapped in a crocheted shawl, reached the top of the attic steps.

"You naughty kiddies!" she said, smiling

brightly, shaking a finger in playful reproof. " Hiding up here in the cold! Come on downstairs by
the fire. Martha has made hot chocolate. We'll
have a nice little game of hearts."

II

It was chilly in the studio. The children huddled
together in a circle on the floor. They hadn't dared
to turn on the lights for fear of being discovered.
A candle burned in an ash tray. Its flickering glow
played over four excited faces. Kit and Gay and
Jamie looked at Barbara.

" We'll run away," she began, trying to make her
voice sound confident in spite of the way that her
heart was thumping against her ribs.

" All of us? " Gay asked, forgetting Aunt Lola
and the dove-gray car in the excitement of an adventure.

" All of us," Barbara said, her eyes very wide
and frightened in her pale face.

" ' Chips,' too? " Jamie asked the question anxiously, the small yellow dog hugged tight against his
chest.

" ' Chips,' too," Barbara said almost gaily.
" Why, Jamie Thorne, do you think we could ever
leave ' Chips ' ? "

" Whoopee! "

Kit's hand against Jamie's mouth muffled the
joyous shout.

"Shut up!" he said sternly. "Do you want the relations to hear?"

Kit's warning made them feel like conspirators planning some monstrous deed. They huddled closer together and talked in quick breathless whispers.

"Where are we going?" Jamie asked, not caring very much since " Chips " was going too.

"We're going to 'Uncle Stephen.'" There, it was out. And it didn't sound crazy at all. It sounded like a sensible thing to do.

"Did he invite us?" Gay asked eagerly, her warm color deepening. "Uncle Stephen," who sent lovely presents, had always been a romantic figure to Gay.

"No," Barbara was forced to admit. "We're just going anyway."

"But Babs," worried thoughtful Kit, "shouldn't you write to ask him? Or telegraph or something?"

"It's better if he sees us." Barbara was sure of that. Certainly " Uncle Stephen " could never resist the charms of Kit and Gay and Jamie. . . . "A crusty old bachelor!" . . . She didn't believe it. His letter sounded so nice. . . .

"Four of us are quite a lot." Kit's brow wore an anxious frown. "Do you suppose he'll have enough beds?"

"Uncle Stephen is rich," Gay said with easy assurance. "He sends such lovely presents." Her

hazel eyes dreamed into the shadows. "Maybe,"
she said, " he'll buy me a squirrel coat."

"Greedy!" Kit said scornfully. "Always thinking of presents!"

Gay's red lips trembled. She nestled closer to
Kit.

"I wouldn't care if he didn't," she said, relin-
quishing for Kit's sake her dream of a squirrel coat.
"I wouldn't care,—if he'll let us stay together."

"Stout fella'," Kit said softly, and Gay was restored to favor.

"I wouldn't expect him to keep us always," Barbara continued. "Four is quite a lot. But he's a
lawyer and he can tell us what to do. I know he
will help us. He said he would." She drew "Uncle Stephen's" letter from her blouse and read the
concluding sentence .   .   .   "'If a crusty old
bachelor can be of assistance, please let him know
at once.' . . . Doesn't that sound sort of
friendly and nice?"

They agreed that it did. Even Kit was reassured. The frown smoothed itself out and his face
slowly brightened. Barbara felt more confident.
She saw "Uncle Stephen," a nice old man, telling
them what to do. They needed a champion. Father
would have approved. It seemed a sensible idea.

Barbara's spirits lifted, tinting her cheeks with a
wild-rose flush, waking the stars in her eyes. The
children shared her confidence. They had always
followed her blindly in and out of childish misadven-

tures. They relaxed comfortably, feeling sure that Babs would " find a way."

" Where does ' Uncle Stephen ' live ? " Gay asked, hoping it would be some enchanting far off place.

" Near Philadelphia."

" That isn't so far."   Gay felt disappointed. Florida was lovely. She had been there with Aunt Lola before.   Palm trees and people smartly dressed, and bathing in the winter. But it was fun to be running away. . . .

" It's not right in the city," Kit said. " Don't you remember ? We looked it up on a map. It's far enough. Have we any money ? How will we get there, Babs ? "

" Hitch-hike," Jamie said promptly. " I'll bet we could, as easy as anything." His face was bright and excited. All of his freckles shone.

" Or we could dress up like gypsies," Gay, always dramatic, suggested. " And dance and play on tambourines and people would give us money."

Gypsies ! Barbara felt a pain in her heart. . . . " Once upon a time there was a gypsy boy who loved very dearly a little gypsy girl." . . . But she couldn't think about Bruce. She kept seeing Kit's face streaked with tears and Jamie looking at " Chips " and Gay growing up into a silly little peacock like Aunt Lola's horrid Gwen. She had to take care of the children. . . .

" I have some money," she said, swallowing hard

to banish the lump in her throat. She showed it to
them, a very slim roll of bills, provided by Great-
aunt Josephine's check.

It looked like a fortune. The children's eyes widened. They felt like millionaires.

"When are we going?" Gay asked, her voice
fluting high with excitement.

"To-morrow morning."

That made it seem real and frightening but very
thrilling, too.

"Won't we tell anybody, Babs?" Jamie wanted
to know.

"No, indeed." Barbara was firm. "We'll go
early in the morning before anybody is up."

"But the train doesn't leave until eight o'clock,"
Kit reminded her. "They'd miss us by that time,
sure. And Jim Bush, at the station, probably
wouldn't sell us tickets if he thought we were running away."

She hadn't thought of that. The pink faded out
of her cheeks. Here was a problem, indeed. Her
spirits drooped. The children felt it. If Babs was
discouraged, there was no hope. They pressed
closer together, subdued and defeated, feeling that
the grown-up world was in hostile league against
them.

It was Martha who solved the problem. She
came into the studio with a warning about taking
cold. The warning was merely an excuse. She
wanted to be near them this last evening together.

The four little Thornes had wormed their way into Martha's grim affections. They were entirely right about it. Martha considered them amusing and handsome and " too smart to live."

" You're up to somethin'," she said.

Martha had lived with them before Mother died. She had been there to welcome them when they returned to the gray-shingled house after two years of being " parcelled out." She knew, by a dozen familiar signs, when they were " up to something."

Martha was a familiar friend. They knew that Martha loved them. They told her about it, Barbara taking the lead, the children interrupting. They drew her into the circle and talked away her objections. Their young arms around her neck made her, in spite of her common-sense, an ally to be trusted.

" I oughtn't to listen." Martha's Yankee conscience battled against her affections. " I ought to go right in the house this minute and tell them what you're up to."

" But you won't," Barbara said confidently, her cheek against Martha's. " You won't do any such thing."

" No, I suppose I won't." Martha surrendered herself unconditionally to the charms of the four Thornes. " There's no fool like an old fool. I won't do any such thing."

They told her about the problem of getting away

in the morning. Martha considered, her forehead
smocked in a frown.

"Jake Preble drives his truck to New Bedford
Thursday mornings," Martha said after an interval
of thought. "Early, though. He leaves around
five o'clock."

To-morrow was Thursday morning. It seemed
an act of providence.

"Will he take us?" They shouted the question
together, forgetting to be cautious, their spirits lifting again.

"He will if I tell him to," Martha said grimly.
"I know enough about that bantam rooster to have
him run out of town."

Barbara could scarcely believe what she heard!
Martha, consistently upright, a member of the
Methodist church, was thinking in terms of black-
mail!

"What will I tell them?" she asked when the
joyous din had subsided.

"Them" meant the relations. Martha's voice
was frosty. She had her opinion of them. They
treated her like a "hired girl." She considered herself one of the family. It pleased her because the
children had appealed to her against them. It
helped her wounded pride.

"We'll leave a note," Barbara said. "We'll tell
them we've gone to Uncle Stephen. They don't
know where he lives. That will give us time. But
Martha," she added, a shadow slipping across her

vivid face, " I'm afraid it won't be pleasant for you.
They'll make a dreadful scene. They'll probably
explode."

" Don't you mind about that." The light of bat-
tle flamed in Martha's eyes. " I'll speak my mind
and pin on my hat and leave."

They fell upon her with strangling hugs.

" You're an angel, Marthy-Ann," Barbara whispered gratefully, her arm around Martha's neck.

" I'm an idiot!" Martha pushed the children
away. Her voice sounded scolding and cross. " I'll
probably live to regret it. But you have a way about
you." She tucked in a hairpin and smoothed her
starched print frock. " There's no fool like an old
fool! I'm goin' to see Jake Preble."

III

Barbara lay, wide awake, in the low carved bed
that Father had made. Gay, curled beside her, was
fast asleep, worn out by excitement and plans. The
alarm clock ticked very loudly on a chair beside the
bed. It was set for four. Martha had " managed "
Jake Preble. They were to leave at five o'clock in
the morning.

Everything was arranged. The children, quaking
for fear they would be discovered, had hidden their
luggage in the studio. Kit had gone to the station
for time-tables and schedules. Sitting together on
the sofa in the attic, a quilt around their shoulders,

Kit's lantern lighted beside them, he and Barbara had marked the way they would go:—from New Bedford to Boston on the train, from Boston to Philadelphia. By seven o'clock to-morrow night they would be at Uncle Stephen's.

For the children's sake, Barbara had suppressed her uncertainties and doubts. She had made running away seem sensible and easy, an exciting sort of adventure. Now, lying awake in the low carved bed, with the rain falling outside and the wind in the willows singing a mournful song, the doubts and uncertainties could no longer be suppressed. Grim, frightening shadows, they trooped in an endless procession through her head.

It was impolite to be running away. The relations meant to be kind. Aunt Lola had come all the way from Florida. Uncle Herbert was neglecting his business and missing football games. Cousin Julia had left Cousin Will to the uncertain mercies of a French-Canadian maid. It was especially kind of them since they had never approved of Mother marrying Father and having four children and living "like a gypsy" as though she hadn't been properly brought up and sent every Sunday of her life to the Congregational church. It was appallingly impolite to leave them and run away.

The money troubled her, too. Was it stealing to use Aunt Josephine's check for the purpose of running away? Aunt Josephine would say that it was. "What can you expect?" she would say. "They've been brought up like heathen!" She wouldn't blame them so much. She would blame Father's happy-go-lucky way of letting them do as they pleased. It seemed a treachery to Father. But, deep in her heart, she knew that Father would approve. He wanted the children to be happy. He had promised that they should never be "parcelled out" again.

What would Uncle Stephen think? His letter had been so friendly. . . . "If a crusty old bachelor can be of assistance, please let him know at once." . . . He had called her his "little fillette." It was a caressing, intimate word. A "crusty old bachelor" wouldn't have thought of such lovely things to write. Perhaps he was lonely and wanted some children. Hers, she thought, were especially attractive. Surely he would appreciate the charms of Kit and Jamie and Gay.

And Bruce? What would he think? She moved the hand which wore his ring and heard through the falling rain the tinkle of the heart. It would be lovely to be with Bruce. She loved him so much, his golden brown hair, his teasing ways, his eyes that were as deeply blue as the sky on a frosty night. . . .

"And every morning for breakast I'll sing you a brand-new song."

"Bruce! . . . A new one every day!"

"And a special one for Sundays." . . .

Thinking of Bruce, she felt warm and drowsy and

not afraid any more. Darling Bruce! She told herself a story . . . "Once upon a time there was
a gypsy boy. . . ." The sound of the rain was
pleasant now. Doubts and uncertainties vanished.
She nestled close against Gay. . . . "The flute
knew only one song—'I love you, pretty gypsy girl
with the roses in your hair. . . .'"

She could hear the song of the silver flute if she
kept very breathless and still, showers of sprinkling
silver notes, thin and high and sweet.

"I love you," the silver notes sang through her
drowsy mind, charming away doubts and uncertainties, hushing the fear in her heart. "I love
you, pretty gypsy girl with the roses in your
hair. . . ."

Barbara's lashes drooped. She sighed and was
fast asleep.

Part Two

I

STEPHEN DRAKE, in an evening shirt and well-pressed trousers braced with black and white suspenders, stood before a mirror tying with fumbling fingers a narrow black silk tie. The mirror was set in a wardrobe carved with oak leaves and acorns and opulent bunches of grapes. All of the furniture in the large high-ceilinged room was of walnut and similarly carved. It was a man's room, unmistakably. The rugs, the window hangings, the counterpane on the bed were a dull terra-cotta shade, rich in texture, vaguely depressing. In the grate in the veined marble fireplace burned a small cannel coal fire. Henry always started the bedroom fires the first day of November.

Unmistakably it was the room of a man of orderly habits and a studious turn of mind. Things were precisely arranged, the brushes on the dresser, the dressing gown folded across the back of the chair beside the hearth, the slippers warming before the fire. Books, pushed together by bronze elephants, stood on the bedside table. Books, handsomely bound, filled the shelves between the windows. A teakwood table near the fire held the requisite equipment for smoking. No ashes lay in the lacquered trays or on the tidy hearth.

There was but one unusual note in the subdued symphony of the room. Above the fireplace hung a painting all color and sunlight, red rocks, blue sea, distant rust colored sails, a girl, slim and graceful, with the wind blowing her skirt against her bare brown legs. The painting made you wonder about the tall erect man, gray at the temples, tying a neat silk tie into a neat silk bow.

Henry wondered about him. But Henry's musings had nothing to do with the painting above the fireplace. That, through long acquaintance, had become familiar and accustomed. Sometimes when he was lighting the fire, Henry paused to look at the painting and a wistful expression crept into his eyes. Henry, in the far distant days of his sprightly youth, had seen rust-colored sails and bare brown legs and water the same bright blue. He had been a steward on a liner before he married Sarah.

But the painting was not in Henry's thoughts tonight as he stood beside Stephen, holding his dinner coat with the sleeves arranged just so. Mister Stephen was taking great pains with the tie, he thought, doing it over and over, which wasn't his usual way. You'd think he was going courting. Perhaps Sarah was right. Perhaps Mister Stephen was going to marry that pale Miss Emily Trent. Looked like it, inviting her and her father for dinner to-night and tying his tie five times. Well, he wished them joy. Perhaps Miss Trent wouldn't look so peaked when she'd been decently fed for a while. . . .

" How does it look? " Stephen asked, patting the neat silk bow.

" Splendid, sir." No hint of what he was thinking appeared in Henry's parchment face, fringed with side whiskers neatly trimmed. He didn't, as he expressed it, " take liberties," although he and Sarah had lived with the family since before Stephen was born. " Splendid, sir," he repeated, as Stephen seemed about to wreck the bow and make another attempt.

" I'll take your word for it, Henry." Stephen smiled and slipped his arms into the coat.

" Will there be anything else, sir? " Henry asked when the coat had been adjusted to their mutual satisfaction.

" No, thank you," Stephen answered absently.

" Have you everything, sir? " Henry felt responsible. Mister Stephen wasn't himself to-night. When a man was thinking of marriage, he was apt to be absent-minded.

" Everything's ship-shape."

" Then I'll be getting downstairs." Henry, spare and neat and elderly, moved with measured tread toward the door. He paused there as though he meant to say something further. Then, apparently changing his mind, he stepped out into the hall and quietly closed the door.

Alone in the room, Stephen was conscious of irritation. Henry had observed his uneasiness, he thought, lighting a cigarette with hands that were not quite steady. Perhaps Henry suspected that he had made up his mind to ask Emily Trent to marry him. He pictured Henry telling Sarah and the other servants how he had fussed with his tie. They would fancy that he was in love,—in the manner of movie lovers to whom they were devoted. They would joke about it, perhaps. His dignity was offended.

Was he in love with Emily Trent? Stephen considered the question gravely as he paced back and forth across the terra-cotta rugs. He admired her very much, was touched by her devotion to her father, enjoyed being with her. There was, in Emily, a quality of serenity as rare as it was charming. He saw her moving through his house, always serene and gracious, her head, with its braids of light brown hair, lifted in the gently dignified way he admired. The picture pleased him. She would fit smoothly into the orderly pattern of his life.

But he wasn't in love with her, not love as the poets described it, a sweet insanity, a madness of the senses. It was not youthful ardor which had caused his difficulty with the tie. Nor was it the fear of being refused. He was confident that Emily would accept his offer of marriage. Why not? She was well over thirty. And living alone with her father was certainly not too pleasant. Professor Trent, a former instructor at the University, was an eccentric old chap who devoted his time to translating the more obscure Greek and Latin poets. He was interesting, taken in very small doses, but Emily must find him trying at times.

Her path through life had not been strewn with roses. She and her father lived a pinched sort of existence in a small apartment on the outer fringe of Rittenhouse Square. The apartment was restful and charming but Stephen, always sensitive to his surroundings, understood the contriving, the private pinching, the ekeing out of a slender income which made possible the flowers, the wood for the open fire, the simple well-served dinners. He could do a great deal for Emily. And he knew that she admired him, even loved him perhaps, in her gentle dignified way. Emily would accept him. He was quite certain of that.

No, it was not youthful ardor or fear of being refused which caused his present uneasiness. It was, he admitted it reluctantly, a fantastic dread of changes. His life was well-ordered and satisfying. He enjoyed his work in the law firm of Van Wyck, Penrose and Drake, an old established firm in which his grandfather had been the original Drake. Aunt Edith, his father's widowed sister, capably managed his house. He had his books, his friendships, an occasional concert or play, golf or riding when he felt the need of exercising out of doors. He was content with things as they were.

But would he continue to be content? Stephen frowned thoughtfully at the tip of his cigarette. He was getting on—forty his last birthday. An elderly bachelor, he had observed, was a pathetic sort of figure. Aunt Edith was sixty-eight. His sister Natalie, twelve years younger than he, was married. He didn't want to be left alone in the house which had sheltered three generations of Drakes. Nor did he want things changed. That, he admitted to himself, was his reason for asking Emily to marry him. She was the one woman of his acquaintance who, he felt, would make no attempt to reorganize his life.

Did this dread of change mean he was getting old? Stephen crossed to the wardrobe mirror and gravely inspected himself. He didn't look old. His figure was trim and erect. He had—thank God!— no sign of a middle-aged paunch. The gray at his temples was an inherited trait, as was his olive skin, the modelling of his rather handsome nose, his gray eyes deeply set under straight dark brows. He was, unmistakably, a Drake, the grandson of old Stephen whose portrait hung in the library downstairs.

He was not unattractive, he decided, taking stock of himself. It was strange that he had never known a real romance. He had a greater capacity for it than even his most intimate friends suspected. But something had held him back from headlong plunges into amorous adventures. His clear-thinking mind, perhaps, his reserve, his fear of making himself ridiculous. Tradition, he supposed. "A Drake is always a gentleman." Something of the sort.

Only once in his life had he had a glimpse of romance. His eyes turned to the painting above the fireplace. She had never known how ardently he loved her. "A Drake is always a gentleman" and her husband had been his friend. She, perhaps, was the true reason why he had never known a real romance. He had looked for her, and never found her, in the women he had known.

Stephen walked to the fireplace and, crossing his arms on the mantel, looked up at the girl with the wind blowing her skirt against her bare brown legs. How lovely she had been. That was a long time ago. Almost eighteen years. He had not seen her since. He knew that she was dead. He had never forgotten her vivid face, her soft brown hair, the dimple that woke when she smiled.   .   .   .

A knock at the door brought him back from the past.

" Come in," he called, turning from the painting with the strange fear that the intruder, whoever it was, might learn from his position the story he never had told.

The intruder was Aunt Edith. She was a large, handsome woman who had been known in her youth as " beautiful Edith Drake." But that, too, was a long time ago. Aunt Edith, now, was comfortably stout with waved white hair, the handsome Drake nose and a fair smooth complexion. Her gown of heavy black silk conformed to an out-of-date style and the garnets which bound her throat and wrists were set in filigreed bands of gold.

Aunt Edith did not toady to fashion. She was a Drake by birth and a Van Wyck by marriage. That fortunate combination assured her of a prominent place on patroness lists and the boards of charitable organizations. She was not obliged to be " smart," a word she deplored, or to follow the latest fads in living.

Her customary manner of assurance was somewhat shaken to-night.

" You aren't ill, are you, Stephen? " she asked when she had closed the door.

" Of course not. Why? " Stephen, again, was conscious of irritation. He was certainly, he told himself, in a beastly mood to-night.

" You were so long coming down." Aunt Edith's fingers twisted a chain studded with star-shaped garnets. " Natalie and Robert are here."

" I supposed they were. I heard the piano."

Aunt Edith was uneasy, too, he thought. Her fingers twisting the chain told him that, the flush in her smooth plump cheeks. As always, he found it difficult to discuss intimate matters with Aunt Edith. The Drakes were not demonstrative. They lived within themselves.

"Are you going to marry Emily Trent?" she asked after a moment of silence.

"I haven't asked her."

"But you mean to."

"Before dinner to-night." Stephen knew a moment of panic. He wished that he might recall the words. Too late. He had committed himself.

"Emily is a sweet unselfish girl. She will make you a suitable wife."

Aunt Edith's voice was not enthusiastic. Women were curious, Stephen thought. She had often advised him to marry. She had no objection to Emily. And yet, now that he was about to follow her advice, she seemed unhappy about it. That was natural, of course. Aunt Edith had been, for many years, the mistress of the house.

"It needn't change things," he said, wanting to reassure her, wanting desperately to reassure himself. "This will always be your home."

"Thank you, my dear." Aunt Edith drew his head down to the level of her lips and lightly kissed his brow. "I hope you will be happy."

The kiss embarrassed them both. They heard, with mutual relief, the sound of a car in the drive.

"There's Thomas." Aunt Edith turned toward the door. "We must go down at once."

Stephen followed her slowly. The feeling of panic returned. That was absurd, he told himself, as he walked down the wide polished stairs. He hadn't been forced into this situation. It was something he wanted to do. But the panic persisted in spite of clear-thinking reason. He felt like a sailor embarking upon a strange uncharted sea.

II

"This is a charming room," Emily said in her gentle voice.

"A bit old-fashioned, I'm afraid." Stephen felt the panic recede. He was soothed by Emily's serenity. She sat so quietly, her hands folded in her lap, her head bound with heavy braids of light brown hair, inclined a little toward him, a listening expression in her odd tea-colored eyes. She was almost pretty to-night, he thought, in the cream-colored lace he particularly admired, her only ornament a coral rose on a slender golden chain.

"It's perfect," Emily continued. "I should hate you"—she smiled to let him know that she could never, under any circumstances, hate him—"if you should change it in any way."

"A perfect setting for you," Stephen said softly. That, at least, was true. The drawing-room with its panelled walls, its rosewood and silver-green brocade, was a perfect setting for Emily. But he wouldn't ask her to marry him here. He would take her into the conservatory after Henry had served the very mild cocktails which Aunt Edith permitted. That would please her, he thought, smiling with masculine tolerance for a woman's romantic whims. The orange trees were in bloom. That would be an excuse.

"Thank you, Stephen." A faint flush crept into her cheeks. "You say nice things so nicely."

Did he mean anything by that? she wondered, frantic with hope and fear. If Stephen asked her to marry him it would make up for everything; the girlhood she had missed, the pinching and contriving, being patient with Father when she wanted to scream and fly into millions of pieces. But she must be calm. She knew that her tranquillity was her greatest charm for Stephen. She spoke of the concert they were to attend this evening after dinner. Her voice was steady and clear as a crystal bell. But her lips felt dry and there was a roaring sound in her ears.

Natalie, tall and graceful in a slim gown of claret velvet, played the piano softly at the other end of the room. She, too, had an olive skin and the Drake gray eyes deeply set under straight dark brows. Robert King, her husband, big and blonde and handsome, lounged against the piano, humming the tune she played, looking over her sleek dark head at Emily and Stephen.

"Nat," he asked, "is Stephen going to marry her?"

"Aunt Edith thinks so." Natalie's satin shod foot pressed the loud pedal for a moment.

"Don't you think we should interfere?" Bob continued, his blue eyes crinkling at the corners.

" He's slipping fast.   Any minute may be too late. Let's yell ' Fire ! ' "

" Goose ! "

" The Owl and the Pussy Cat."   Bob glanced at Professor Trent in his shell-rimmed glasses talking earnestly to Aunt Edith; at Emily, looking up at Stephen, her head attentively tilted, her hands folded in her lap.   " She's purring already," he reported.   " Pussy likes her cream."

" You're scandalous, Bob ! "   Her eyes loved him, his shoulders, his eyes, his crisp blonde hair.   She wanted to feel concerned because Stephen was going to marry Emily Trent.   Emily was so precise and well—" old maidish."   And Stephen was a dear in spite of his quiet orderly ways.   She wanted a little glamour for Stephen.   She and Bob were so happy. Bob !   She felt his love pouring over her, blotting out every thought not centered in themselves.

" Darling ! " she whispered, through light rippling chords.

" Darling ! " he answered, bending to touch her hair.

Half-way down the long room, lighted with crystal wall brackets and a glittering chandelier, Aunt Edith was marooned with Professor Trent on a rosewood sofa upholstered in silver-green brocade. Professor Trent was small and thin and weazened. His evening clothes, greenish with age and smelling faintly of moth balls, hung about him in drooping folds.   But the little professor was not concerned

with his appearance. He had found a listener and
was taking advantage of his good fortune. With
his near-sighted eyes beaming behind the shell-
rimmed glasses, his finger tips pressed together, his
chin dipping at intervals into his too-large collar, he
talked steadily on and on.

Aunt Edith wanted to scream. Wouldn't he ever
stop talking? He was a scholarly man, she knew,
and very much respected. He had managed, somehow, to marry one of the Paynes. But he certainly
was a bore. She thought of the little professor
living here in the house, for of course he would if
Stephen married Emily. Perhaps she would take
the Mediterranean cruise this winter. She hated to
leave her flowers, her bridge, her comfortable room.
But certainly she couldn't stand much of this. She
stiffened her jaws to suppress a yawn which brought
tears into her eyes.

Henry arrived with the cocktails. Emily sipped
hers slowly, taking a very long time. Stephen
fumed with impatience and then, when she had finished, he was uneasy and urged her to have another.

She shook her head. He saw that her hands were
trembling. Dear Emily. Tenderness stirred in his
heart. Aunt Edith was showing Professor Trent
the curios in the crystal and rosewood cabinet.
Natalie and Bob were looking through a pile of
music, entirely absorbed in themselves. It was an
opportune moment to slip away. Stephen turned to
Emily.

"Aunt Edith's orange trees actually bloomed," he said, trying to make his voice sound casual. "The advertisement said they would, but we didn't really believe it. They're quite effective. Would you like to see them?"

"Very much," Emily said faintly.

He was taking her to the conservatory! Did that mean anything? She knew she was acting like a goose. But it meant so much to her. She wanted to be married, to be cared for and secure. She wanted to marry Stephen. She felt herself walking beside him down the wide shadowy hall as though she were moving in a dream. She was afraid she was going to cry or do something embarrassing. Her serenity was gone. Her knees felt weak. There was a humming sound in her ears.

The orange trees stood in painted tubs, small dwarfed trees with glossy green leaves and clusters of wax-like blossoms.

"Lovely!" Emily breathed, hiding her hot face among the moist leaves, smelling the fragrance of the blossoms. Orange blossoms! Surely that was significant.

"Aunt Edith takes great pride in her flowers." Stephen slipped his arm through Emily's, pleased because she liked the conservatory which Natalie said was old-fashioned. They walked among ferns and palms and airily trailing vines; they paused to admire the tasselled fuchias, the begonias falling in lusty cascades of green and red and yellow. A

fountain dripped with a tinkling sound into a shal-
low basin. The rain which had been falling all day,
tapped gently against the enclosing glass. Aunt
Edith's love-birds, in a gilded cage, made small soft
chirping sounds.

"Lovely!" Emily breathed to the carnations, to
the small potted rose tree covered with pink-tipped
buds. If she might stay here always! Her eyes
filled with tears.

"You're crying."

"I'm a goose." She fumbled for her handkerchief, hating herself for crying, wondering what he
thought.

"Let's use mine."

He wiped away her tears with a square of fine
linen which had a pleasant smell. Everything about
him was so exactly right. She wondered how it
would feel to have him kiss her and the color swept
into her cheeks.

Stephen saw the bright pink flush. Perhaps, for
Emily, he was a real romance. The thought surprised him. It had not occurred to him before.
Dear Emily! She looked young and appealing in
the dim light of the conservatory. She would make
him a charming wife. That, he thought, was
enough.

"Emily . . ." He drew her to him, felt her
trembling in his arms. Her cheek, when he touched
it with his hand, was smooth and warm and fragrant. It seemed absurd to him now that he had

ever felt uneasy about asking her to marry him.
"Emily, dear . . ."

There was a sound of footsteps, a discreet warning cough. Emily slipped away from his arms,
stood looking at one of the orange trees, her fingers
touching a cluster of wax-like blossoms. Henry,
spare and elderly and tactful, walked toward them
between the palms and ferns and the airily trailing
vines.

"I beg your pardon, Mister Stephen," he said,
coughing discreetly again. "But there's someone to
see you, sir."

"Callers?" Stephen asked, annoyed at the inter-
ruption.

"Four children."

"Children?"

"They asked especially for you." Henry's face
was solemn and grave. Inside he was bursting with
curiosity. This was an eventful evening. He would
have a great deal to tell Sarah, laid up with neu-
ralgia, and missing all the excitement.

"I can't imagine ——" Stephen's brow was
creased in a puzzled frown. "All right, Henry.
I'll come."

Henry took himself off, pleased and excited inside, his face as stiff as a parchment mask.

"Wait for me here," Stephen said to Emily.
"I'll return as soon as I can"—he lifted her hand
to his lips and added gently—"dear."

He was gone so long! Emily broke off a cluster

of orange blossoms. The petals spilled from her fingers, drifted down to the floor.

III

They stood huddled together in the hall, a weary, worn-looking little group, surrounded by shabby luggage.

Who were they? Stephen wondered as he came from the shadows into the light of the hall chandeliers. He was sure he had not seen them before. And yet the older girl looked familiar. There was something about the shape of her face, the curly brown hair tumbling against her shoulders from under a brown beret.

She detached herself from the group and walked to meet him, a weary but gallant figure, in a velveteen jacket and a pleated skirt.

"Are you Uncle Stephen?" she asked, extending politely a small, very grubby hand.

Uncle Stephen! The name pronounced in a voice husky with weariness caused Stephen's heart to stir strangely. The puzzled frown left his brow.

"Yes," he said, taking the small hand which felt cold and very frightened.

"You couldn't be expected to recognize me." She lifted a pale face set with dark anxious eyes. "You haven't seen me since I was a baby being christened."

"Of course I recognize you," Stephen said gently.

"I would have known you anywhere. You are my little fillette."

There was a sudden bewildering change in the small heart-shaped face. The weariness vanished, the lines of anxiety smoothed themselves out. The wide dark eyes shone like misty stars. The red lips smiled, a gay smile that woke a sleeping dimple.

"You called me that," she said. "That's why we ran away."

CHAPTER II

I

AUNT EDITH, wrapped in jet-trimmed velvet with a lacy scarf festooned about her head, came into the library as the clock chimed eleven.

"Well, Stephen?" she said.

The "Well" demanded an explanation. Stephen rose from a chair beside the fire.

"Did you enjoy the concert?" he asked, hoping to turn Aunt Edith's mind from the disturbing events of the evening. He was in no mood for explanations. He wished, very fervently, that Aunt Edith had gone directly to bed.

"I can't say that I did." Aunt Edith settled into a chair and unfastened the jet-trimmed wrap. "I may be a conceited old woman," she added dryly, "but I don't flatter myself to the extent of believing that I was an acceptable substitute for you."

"I'm sorry," Stephen said briefly. He seemed preoccupied. Aunt Edith was sure he had not read a word of the book which he held in his hand.

"It was rude, Stephen," she said. "Emily felt it, I'm sure."

"I'm sorry," he said again. This time the words sounded more sincere. Emily! He had forgotten her entirely. She had no part in the thoughts which had occupied his mind since his unexpected guests had been fed and put to bed. He made a mental note to send Emily flowers the first thing in the morning. "I think she will understand," he said.

"You're optimistic." A grim smile hovered about Aunt Edith's lips. Stephen, she thought, had much to learn about women. "Who are these children?" she asked.

"Their name is Thorne." Stephen paced back and forth across the hearth. "Barbara is my godchild."

"Barbara? The older girl?"

"Yes."

"How old is she?"

"Eighteen."

"Indeed!" Aunt Edith seemed surprised. "You have never mentioned a godchild," she continued, after a pause.

"There has been no occasion."

"There is an occasion now." Aunt Edith's fingers twisted the chain set with star-shaped garnets. "I try not to pry into your affairs. But, four children! Or rather three children and a young girl. Well, I am only human, Stephen."

"Of course." Stephen smiled. "You are entitled to an explanation."

"Stop pacing, please." Aunt Edith returned the

smile. " We are much alike," she said complacently.
" We hate to have our plans interrupted. We hate
to be jolted out of our comfortable ruts."

" I suppose so." Stephen dropped into the armchair and stretched out his feet to the fire. Very
briefly he told her the story of Barbara's christening.

" Odd sort of people," Aunt Edith observed,
—" asking a stranger to be godfather for their
child."

" They were charming," Stephen said gently.
" Both of them were artists."

" Oh ! " Aunt Edith said, as though that explained the odd request. She had seen artists wandering through the Academy, young men with
longish hair, girls in smocks with a great many
bright colored beads. " One doesn't think of artists
having children. Not in quantities," she added.

" They do, I suppose." Stephen described
Christopher Thorne as he remembered him. He
talked about the dark-eyed baby that Barbara had
been. He spoke of the interval he had spent with
them in a village in southern France. Of Barbara's
mother he said little. It was no concern of Aunt
Edith's if he had loved a slender dark-eyed girl
whose name was Barbara Thorne. He could not
speak of it lightly. It was a story he never had
told.

" Have they no relatives ? " she asked when he
had concluded the sketch with the death of Christopher Thorne.

"Too many relatives," Stephen answered. "That seems to be the trouble."

"What do you mean?"

"The children don't want to be separated. They were, for a time,—after the mother died. That's why they ran away."

"Ran away!" Aunt Edith's face wore a horrified expression.

"The relatives are in Provincetown. The children ran away from them in a truck."

"I never heard of such a thing!" Aunt Edith bristled with indignation. "They must be distracted. Have you wired them? What sort of people are they?"

"Highly respectable, I should say." Again Stephen smiled. "Barbara spoke of an Uncle Herbert. A relative named Uncle Herbert must be a respectable person."

Aunt Edith looked distressed.

"I can't see that it's a matter for making jokes," she said, her fingers twisting the chain.

"It isn't." The smile vanished. Stephen's expression was grave and troubled again. "They seem to think I can help them. I have sent Barbara a gift every year and I wrote to her when I heard of her father's death. I wish I could help them. They're nice youngsters. But what in the world can I do?"

"You can send them back to their relatives," Aunt Edith said firmly. "To-morrow."

" Not to-morrow, Aunt Edith."

" Why not? "

" They're completely exhausted." Stephen re-membered Kit's white face, the circles of weariness chalked under Barbara's eyes. " They'll have to rest for a day or two."

A word of protest rose to Aunt Edith's lips. She was having a luncheon to-morrow. Four children would be hard to explain. But then, this was Stephen's house. The protest dissolved slowly and became a sigh.

" Where is that yellow dog? " she asked, recall-ing the fifth member of the party.

Stephen looked embarrassed. He looked, Aunt Edith thought, just about twelve years old. His voice, when he answered the question, was hesitating and guilty.

" He's tucked into bed with Jamie."

" Stephen! A dog in one of the beds! "

" Bessie washed him. She used carbolic-acid soap." A smile, half provoked, half amused, touched the corners of Stephen's lips. " He was clean and very fragrant when we tucked him into bed."

The smile disturbed Aunt Edith. What was the matter with Stephen? Why was he so concerned about these bedraggled children? A dog in one of the beds! She felt very uneasy.

" You aren't thinking of keeping them? " she asked.

"Keeping them! The children, you mean?"

She nodded.

"Of course not!" Stephen's expression was so startled that Aunt Edith was reassured. "What would I do with four children on my hands?"

"I wondered." Aunt Edith collected her wrap and her scarf, her gloves and her jet beaded bag. "You've had a disturbing evening," she said as she rose from the chair. "Dogs and runaway children and carbolic-acid soap. You'd better go to bed and think no more about them. And in the morning," she added, pausing at the door, "you'd better call Emily and apologize. There are some things a woman finds it difficult to be understanding about."

What did she mean by that? Aunt Edith seemed to feel that Emily needed defending.

Aunt Edith did not explain.

"Good-night," she said and closed the library door.

II

Emily ——

Stephen raked the coals in the grate and returned to the deep soft chair. He had been rude. He hadn't, he remembered now, returned to the conservatory and the love-birds and the blossoming orange trees. He had had dinner with the children in the old schoolroom upstairs. But he thought Emily would understand.

He would send her flowers in the morning. No, he would take them himself, her favorite white lilacs, and he would tell her the things he had meant to say this evening before the children arrived. What had he told her? How far had he gone? It embarrassed him to realize that he couldn't remember distinctly.

The second part of Aunt Edith's advice he found himself entirely unable to follow. He thought a great deal about the children as he sat in the armchair beside the fire. They were amusing youngsters. Tired as they were, a little awed by their surroundings, he had enjoyed them to-night. Fragments of their conversation returned to him and the smile, half provoked, half amused, touched the corners of his lips. . . .

"You aren't nearly as old as we thought you'd be." That was Gay. "You belong to Bab really, of course, but we adopted you for an uncle."

"Four is quite a lot." That was Christopher-Kit. "If you haven't room, I can sleep on a couch. We don't want to bother you, sir."

"He's no particular kind of a dog." That was Jamie, a sturdy little fellow with reddish-brown hair and freckles all over his face. "But he has a sort of a nice disposition and never any fleas."

"You called me that. That's why we ran away. . . ."

Barbara. That was her mother's name. The daughter was very like the Barbara he had loved,

the same heart-shaped face, the soft brown hair, the
dimple that woke when she smiled. Younger, of
course, more slightly built, not so vivid, perhaps.
But sufficiently like her to arouse disturbing memories of the adventure in southern France.

That, he thought, his eyes on the glowing coals,
was the only real adventure he had ever known. He
had forgotten, for a time, that he was Stephen
Drake, had shared the happy-go-lucky existence of
Christopher Thorne and his charming dark-eyed
wife. He was young then, just out of college. He
had thought all of life might be like that—work,
congenial friends, new places to see, a wife with the
gift of laughter.

It hadn't been, of course. He had been restless,
for a time, when he returned home. He had planned
vacation adventures, a voyage on a tramp schooner,
a walking trip through Nova Scotia, a winter jaunt
through Italy and Spain. He had accomplished
none of them. He had spent his vacations with
Aunt Edith and Natalie at Cape May or Watch
Hill or Poland Springs. He had never recaptured
the glamor of that spring in southern France.

Even the war had failed him. He had, through
no fault of his own, spent the time in Washington
behind a quartermaster's desk. Gradually the restlessness had disappeared. Life had arranged itself
into a neat pattern, orderly and satisfying. Some
men were born for adventure. He had probably
been in the cradle, Stephen told himself, a sedate

and dignified lawyer, gray at the temples even then, insisting that his meals should be served exactly on time, that his daily outings follow the conventional route of well-bred perambulators.

He was, on the whole, content with his orderly life. Only at rare intervals did he feel that, somehow, he had been cheated. It was years since he had experienced the restlessness which troubled him to-night.

The children were responsible, he thought; Barbara with her soft brown hair and the dimple at the left corner of her mouth. When he had returned them to their relatives, life would go on the usual way. Very nearly the usual way. There would be Emily, of course. But Emily would not attempt to make changes. White lilacs. He wondered if the florist had them at this season of the year. . . .

" Uncle Stephen . . ."

Stephen's eyes turned from the glowing coals to the library door which had opened so softly that he had not been conscious of the sound. Barbara, in a rose-colored kimono, her hair tumbled about her face, stood, hesitating, just inside the room.

" Why aren't you asleep? " Stephen asked. " It's after midnight, young lady."

" I know." She pushed back the tumbling hair. " There are so many clocks. I heard them striking all over the house."

" Haven't you slept at all? "

" Not a single wink. I came down to see if you

were here." She walked to the fire, pajama legs showing under the kimono, her feet tucked into slippers with rose-colored pom-poms. " I want to talk, Uncle Stephen."

" But Barbara ——"

" Couldn't you call me Babbie? " she asked. She was standing beside him now. She lifted her face and he saw a wistful expression in her wide dark eyes. " Father always did." Father and Bruce, she thought. She did not mention Bruce.

" Babbie ——" He smiled. " Is that better? "
Her face brightened.

" Much better," she said. " Especially the smile."

" What shall we talk about? " he asked when she had curled herself into the chair beside the fire.

" I want to explain." She looked at him gravely. " I haven't very well. I'm not sure that I can."

" Don't try to-night." Stephen sat in the chair which Aunt Edith had occupied on the opposite side of the hearth. She looked so young, he thought, curled in the deep soft chair, younger than she had seemed earlier in the evening. It was the kimono, perhaps, and the tumbled soft brown hair.

" I'd rather." Her eyes were troubled, chalked underneath with circles of fatigue. " I couldn't sleep. I wondered what you were thinking."

" I've been thinking," Stephen said gravely, " that it was wrong to run away."

" I suppose it was," she said with a soft little

sigh. " But I didn't know what else to do. You
see "—the wide dark eyes asked him to understand
—" it was because of Kit. He cried so, Uncle
Stephen. I'd never seen Kit cry like that."

" Why? " Stephen asked gently. " Can you tell
me about it? "

She told him of Uncle Herbert and the boys who
were too healthy and active for Kit.

" Kit isn't very strong. The doctors say he will
never entirely outgrow the limp. And he's so brave
about it." Her voice was warm with love for Kit.
" Kit's so—so splendid, Uncle Stephen."

" I'm sure he is," Stephen said. " I knew at once
that Kit was a splendid chap."

Barbara's face lighted swiftly with pleasure.
Uncle Stephen seemed to understand. It was easier,
now, to tell him about the relatives. She talked
eagerly, a torrent of words. She wanted so desperately to make him understand.

Stephen watched the changing expressions in the
small pale face framed in curly soft brown hair.
Her detached view of people amazed and startled
him. She might have been twice her age, he
thought. She was too young to be so tolerant and
so reasonable. She made him see them clearly,
these relatives who meant to be kind but couldn't
understand. He found himself resenting the mature
expression which had settled into her eyes. She
had known too much responsibility, too much sadness, he thought. It occurred to him that charming

Christopher Thorne might not have been an entirely reliable parent.

"Why did you come to me?" he asked when she had finished and sat looking into the fire. He wished that she wasn't so small and forlorn and appealing. He found it hard to be severe.

"Your letter was friendly." Her lashes swept up from her cheeks. Again Stephen's heart stirred strangely. There was something familiar and disconcerting in the way her lashes lifted. "I carried it in my blouse," she confessed, suddenly shy.

"You did?" He was touched by her confidence, a little provoked, as well. They were nice youngsters, all of them. But what in the world could he do?

She nodded. A flush that matched the kimono crept into her cheeks.

"You didn't sound like a 'crusty old bachelor,'" she said, her lashes drooping again. "Besides, there was no one else. Father had no close relations. There was only Mother's family. And they just think we're a duty. They don't approve of us at all."

"What did you think I could do?" Stephen had left the chair and was pacing across the hearth.

"I thought, maybe, if you'd write to them about it, they'd let me keep the children in Provincetown." Her voice was eager. Hope had lighted the dark stars in her eyes. "You're a lawyer, aren't you, Uncle Stephen?"

"Yes," he answered, wondering what lay behind the question.

"They have a great respect for lawyers," she said. "Aunt Lola sends for hers no matter what happens and so does Aunt Josephine. Of course they thought it was crazy when I asked them because they think I'm no older than Gay. But, maybe, if you thought it was a sensible plan ——"

"I don't." Stephen was surprised at the vehemence in his voice. "You're too young to assume the responsibility for three children. You're no more than a child yourself."

"I'm not!" The rose flush deepened. The dark eyes flashed. The words came in a rushing torrent again. "I'm eighteen. And older than that inside. I've taken care of the children always. At least," she added with a little sob in her voice, "ever since Mother died. Father was a darling. He was a most amusing parent. But he didn't know about sore throats and upset stomachs and tantrums and temperatures. I do, Uncle Stephen. I could take care of them. I ——" She had meant to say that she was old enough to be engaged to Bruce. But perhaps Uncle Stephen would think that was crazy, too. She pressed her hands together and felt the ring with the small gold heart cutting into her hand. . . .

"Barbara. Babbie, dear ——"

"You're like the rest of them," she said stormily. "I thought you would understand. Your letter was so friendly and nice. I ——" She knew it was useless to talk. Tears caught in a lump in her throat. She buried her head in her arms and under the rose kimono her shoulders trembled with sobs.

Stephen wanted to comfort her. She was too young to endure such suffering, so young and, somehow, so brave.

"Babbie"—he said—"don't cry so—please." Barbara's daughter! It was strange that she should be here. He wished he might help her, for that other Barbara's sake. But what in the world could he do?

Barbara grew quieter.

"I'm sorry, Uncle Stephen." She lifted a face damp with tears. "I—I'm dreadfully tired."

"Of course you are." Stephen returned to his chair beside the hearth. "I don't mind your crying," he said, "but I do mind your being unhappy."

"Do you?"

"Of course."

"That helps." Her head drooped against the back of the chair. "That's a very comforting thought."

Presently the curly head lifted again.

"Are you going to send us back?" she asked and the expression that was not childish settled into her eyes.

"I'm afraid I must."

"Yes." She sighed. "I suppose you must." Then, after a moment, "When?"

"Not for a day or two."

"Really!" Her face brightened a little.

"You're tired." She looked so dreadfully tired, he thought. He wanted to keep her there—not permanently, of course, just until she had rested. "I want you to stay for a day or two. I have wired to Provincetown."

"Thank you." She smiled shakily. "I'll bet they're mad. I'll bet Uncle Herbert exploded."

"Barbara!"

"I'm sorry," she said drowsily. "I haven't a nice disposition. Will your aunt mind very much if we stay?"

"I think not."

"She didn't seem pleased to see us."

"It was a surprise," Stephen said tactfully.

"And we looked a sight. Trains always seem to be dirty."

"You looked very nice when your faces were washed."

"Such a lovely bathroom! We didn't know your home would be so—well, so grand. I've never lived with a butler before. It's an educating experience."

"Henry isn't a real butler. We live very quietly, Barbara. Henry does all sorts of things."

She was silent for a moment, her head drooping against the chair, her eyes watching the fire.

"Uncle Stephen?"

"Yes?"

"You needn't answer if this is an impertinent

question. But is the lady who had on the lacy dress a *particular* friend of yours? "

" Miss Trent? She's a very dear friend."

" Gay thought you were engaged to her. Are you, Uncle Stephen? "

Stephen smiled. He wished someone would answer that question for him. It would help him, to-morrow, with the lilacs.

" I have known her for years," he said.

Barbara did not insist upon a more definite answer.

" Gay always thinks people are engaged," she said. " She's a very romantic child."

" Pretty, too."

" Yes." Barbara sighed faintly. " Gay is a little beauty. That's why I wanted to keep her with Kit. She's apt to be dreadfully spoiled. She is so susceptible to impressions."

Again she was quiet for a moment. Then, again, her lashes slowly lifted.

" I'm sorry I said what I did." Her wide dark eyes, sleepy, misted with tears, asked him to forgive her. " You aren't like the others, Uncle Stephen. You're comfortable," she said drowsily, " and very, very nice."

Stephen had difficulty with his voice. He was obliged to cough once or twice before he was able to say:

" That's a nice compliment. Thank you, Babbie dear."

III

Aunt Edith roused from uneasy slumber and switched on the bedside lamp. She felt extremely uncomfortable. It was the almond pudding for dinner, she thought. She ought to know better than to eat Katie's company desserts.

There were no soda tablets in her bathroom, she discovered, moving about in a quilted kimono, fur-topped slippers and a net bonnet tied under her chin to protect her careful marcel. No use to try to wake Bessie, though. She was getting worse every day. Almost as deaf as a post.

That was the trouble with elderly servants, Aunt Edith thought, poking about to make sure there were no soda tablets. They weren't much use in an emergency. Still, Bessie was used to her ways. And she was used to Bessie. She'd hate anyone but Bessie to bring up her breakfast tray. She wouldn't disturb Bessie. She would just slip down to the kitchen and borrow Katie's soda.

She knew, without glancing at the mirror, that she looked ridiculous in the bonnet tied with ribbons under her chin. Like an old pink and white baby. But it was very late. After two o'clock. No one would see her. She opened her bedroom door and stepped out into the hall.

There was a sound of footsteps. Someone was coming upstairs. Aunt Edith would have retreated had not astonishment rooted her to a spot on the hallway carpet. There was Stephen with one of those children in his arms. The older girl. What was her name? Barbara. In her night clothes, too, and slippers with fuzzy pom-poms. Whatever had happened to Stephen? At least, when he saw her, he had the grace to look embarrassed.

They were both embarrassed. Aunt Edith thought of her bonnet and the cold cream on her nose. Stephen smiled as he passed her, a sheepish sort of smile and looked down at the girl asleep in his arms and whispered a cautious "Shh!" He walked on down the hall and opened the door of the room where Bessie had put the two girls to bed. There was something in his expression . . .

"Gracious!" Aunt Edith said and shook her head and buttoned her lips together.

CHAPTER III

I

KIT was ill.

He lay under a damask counterpane in a huge bed propped against pillows that felt cool and smooth and had a pleasant smell. There was a flush in his thin dark cheeks and his hazel eyes burned with a feverish brightness. His voice, when he talked, was a husky croak and he had a pain in his chest.

"Exhaustion," the doctor said. He was a dapper little man with socks and a tie and a handkerchief that matched the stripes in his shirt. He thumped Kit's chest and listened through a stethoscope and thrust a thermometer into his mouth. Then, in the way that doctors have, he immediately asked a question.

"What have you been doing?" he asked, timing Kit's pulse by a watch on a platinum chain.

Stephen answered for Kit who couldn't talk because of the thermometer. Stephen felt that the question was meant for him. Doctor Chase had been the Drake physician for many years. It was natural that he should be curious about the children. He told the story briefly, smiling at Kit propped against the pillows, at Barbara seated beside the bed, looking more rested this morning, he thought, but anxious because Kit was ill.

They were friends of his, Stephen said. They had come to make him a visit. The trip from Provincetown in the rain had been, perhaps, a little too much for Kit.

" Hmm ——" said Doctor Chase.

" Is he very ill? " Barbara asked anxiously. The trip in the rain *had* been too much for Kit. She would never forgive herself if running away had made Kit very ill.

The doctor reassured her.

" A touch of bronchitis," he said, squinting at the thermometer. " Some fever. Nothing to be alarmed about. He needs quiet and rest."

" How long? " Kit croaked from the huge bed.

" Oh, a week or two." Doctor Chase screwed the thermometer into a silver case. " I hope," he added, twinkling at Kit, " you haven't any important engagements."

A week or two! Barbara looked at Uncle Stephen. He was frowning a little, his brows drawn down over his pleasant gray eyes. They were going to be a bother to him. They shouldn't have run away. She sat very still in the stuffed damask chair, feeling extremely unhappy.

"Shall I get a nurse?" Stephen asked.

"Well——" Doctor Chase shook some bright colored pills into an envelope. "Well——" he repeated, considering the question.

"Oh, no, Uncle Stephen," Barbara said. "Nurses are very expensive. I can take care of Kit."

"You!" The doctor twinkled at the small anxious person in the deep damask stuffed chair.

"I always have," Barbara said earnestly, "when Kit has been sick like this. I know just exactly what to do."

"Well!" Doctor Chase seemed surprised. "Stand up," he said. "Let me see if you look like a reliable nurse."

Barbara uncurled herself from the chair. She wished she had pinned in her hair this morning. She wished her skirt was longer. She tried to look grown up and tall.

"Will I do?" she asked.

Doctor Chase, still twinkling, considered that question, too.

"How old are you?" he asked.

"Past eighteen."

The doctor raised a quizzical eyebrow.

"I shouldn't have thought it," he said. He looked at Stephen. He looked at Barbara. His eyebrow lifted again. "Very well," he said, snapping the catch on his leather bag. "Two of these every hour. I'll stop in again this evening."

Doctor Chase took himself off with his leather

case and his handsome tweeds and his watch on a
platinum chain. His eyebrow remained quizzically
lifted as, accompanied by Henry, he walked down
the wide polished stairs.

"I'm sorry," Kit said when the doctor had gone.

"That's all right," Stephen said gently. The
frown vanished. He found it hard to be severe
with Kit. The boy had charming manners and he
looked so completely done in.

"But it isn't all right," Kit persisted. "We're
going to be a bother. We—we shouldn't have
come."

"Don't think about that now."

"I knew we shouldn't." Kit straightened himself
against the pillows. "But Babs made it seem a
sensible idea."

"I'm sure she did," Stephen smiled at Barbara
bringing a glass of water for Kit to take his pills.
Her expression was anxious. There was a pucker,
soft as a wrinkle in silk, between her curving brows.
"Don't worry," he said to Kit. "Get well as fast
as you can."

"I will," Kit promised and then, remembering
his manners, "it's very kind of you, sir."

"Very kind," echoed Barbara. "Isn't he lovely,
Kit?"

Stephen left them together. Extraordinary children, he thought. Too reasonable and grown up for
their years and, at the same time, so delightfully
childish. The boy was a charming lad. He won-

dered if anything could be done about the limp. He
might as well speak to Doctor Chase now while the
children were here.

A clock struck ten as he walked downstairs.
Stephen frowned. He was, already, an hour late at
the office. His daily routine would be upset. A
family, he thought, was certainly distracting. Well,
it wouldn't be for long ——

Aunt Edith stood in the lower hall. Her expression was resigned.

" What did the doctor say? " she asked.

" A touch of bronchitis."

" Oh, dear ! " Aunt Edith sighed and buttoned
her lips together.

The sigh irritated Stephen. It was merely bronchitis, after all. She needn't look as though the
house was smitten with a plague.

" He needs rest and quiet." Stephen found himself apologizing for Kit. " He's a sensitive boy and
not very strong. He has been under a heavy strain."

" Hmm —— " said Aunt Edith and buttoned her
lips again.

" It can't be helped," Stephen said brusquely.
" We can't put a sick child out of the house." But,
after all, it *was* difficult for Aunt Edith. She wasn't
accustomed to children. " You needn't be incon-
venienced," he said more gently. " Barbara will
take care of him."

" Is she competent? " Aunt Edith unbuttoned her
lips to ask.

"I think so." Stephen smiled. "She isn't an ordinary child."

"No," Aunt Edith agreed. She looked at Stephen questioningly. He knew that she was thinking of the meeting, last night, in the upper hall. Should he explain the situation? It wasn't necessary, he decided, feeling vastly relieved.

"Have you called Emily?" Aunt Edith asked, after a moment of silence.

Stephen hadn't. He had meant to, of course. But this morning Kit had been ill. Women were curious, he thought. Aunt Edith, last evening, had not seemed very happy about his marrying Emily. Now she was Emily's champion. It was difficult to explain.

He hadn't time to explain it then. A sudden uproar banished any thought of Emily. It came from the rear of the house, voices, excited squeals, the barking of a dog. A feathered object flew into the hall above their heads. Henry followed, Gay with her brown curls dancing, Jamie flushed and distressed, the small yellow dog in a frenzy of excitement.

"It's one of the birds!" Aunt Edith gasped.

Stephen finally caught it, after a strenuous prolonged chase.

"How did this happen?" he asked when he had restored the frightened bird to Aunt Edith.

Gay looked at Jamie accusingly. Jamie, his ears very red, looked down at the tips of his shoes.

"It was my fault," he mumbled. "I opened the door."

"You shouldn't have, Jamie." Gay wasn't looking at Jamie. She looked at Aunt Edith, an apology in her eyes. "Poor little bird!" she murmured and stroked the ruffled feathers.

The child had a way with her, Stephen thought. She was an artful little minx. Aunt Edith visibly relaxed. Stephen turned to Jamie.

"Why did you open the cage?"

"I just wanted to touch them," Jamie confessed. "I never saw any birds like that—just robins and sparrows and things. 'Chips' never did either, I guess. That's why he barked so loud. And the bird got scared ——"

"Stephen," said Aunt Edith, directing a glance at "Chips," "I simply can't have that ——"

Jamie understood the look. He had seen Cousin Julia look at "Chips" in that threatening sort of way.

"'Chips' doesn't chase birds," he interrupted, lifting round brown eyes to Aunt Edith's frown. "He just never saw any like that before. 'Chips' is polite to birds."

"Better keep him out of the conservatory," Stephen said before Aunt Edith could finish her sentence. "Why don't you and 'Chips' go outdoors?"

"Can we?" Jamie asked eagerly.

How did you amuse children? Stephen wondered.

He knew very little about them. He tried to remember what he had liked when he was twelve
years old. It seemed a long time ago.

"There's a dog house out near the garage," he
said, recalling a Great Dane he once had had.
"You might see if 'Chips' would like to live in it
while you are here."

Jamie's freckled face shone. He clumped upstairs
for his sweater and cap. "Chips" followed, his
feet making scratching sounds on the steps, his tail
frantically wagging.

"I'm so sorry," Gay murmured. "I told Jamie
not to open the cage."

"There's been no harm done, I guess." Aunt
Edith held the bird against her taffeta bosom. "Is
the other one safe?"

"Yes, Mrs. Van Wyck," said Henry, dignified
and solemn in spite of the strenuous chase.

"Henry was wonderful." Gay smiled at Henry
and the smile made him her slave. "The conservatory is lovely." She glanced from Stephen to Aunt
Edith. Her hazel eyes widened with childish delight. "I never saw such perfectly beautiful
flowers."

Little minx! Stephen thought. She had found,
already, the chink in Aunt Edith's armor. He was
not surprised when Aunt Edith said:

"I must cut some flowers for luncheon. Would
you like to help me, Gay?"

"I'd love to," Gay answered, stealing a glance

at Stephen. She looked, he thought, like a little girl who had just given her shoes to an orphan as she walked with Aunt Edith down the hall. "The cunning little orange trees!" he heard her say before the hall door closed.

Orange trees. White lilacs for Emily. The man from Thompson and Gallard's was coming this morning. He must reach some decision in the Arnold case. Stephen glanced at his watch. Almost eleven o'clock! A family, he thought as Henry brought his hat and coat, was certainly distracting!

II

Miss Finch, Stephen's secretary, glanced up from the papers on her desk as Stephen came into his office. Her eyes, behind glasses that pinched on her nose, were two startled questions.

"I'm late this morning," Stephen said, feeling uncomfortably guilty.

"Yes, Mr. Drake." Miss Finch adjusted her paper cuffs. Under her neat blue serge she was bursting with dozens of questions. Mr. Drake was invariably punctual. "You could set the clock by him," she told her married sister with whom she lived. And here he was two hours late! It was as astonishing as a snow storm in July.

"The man from Thompson and Gallard's was here," she said as Stephen began to open the letters placed in a neat pile on his desk.

Stephen glanced up quickly.

"Has he gone?" he asked.

"He waited an hour." Miss Finch primly consulted a pad. "The appointment was for ten o'clock."

"Good Lord!" Stephen groaned. "That was important."

"Yes," said Miss Finch accusingly.

"Families are distracting."

"I beg your pardon, Mr. Drake?"

"I was thinking aloud." Stephen smiled, a smile half amused and half provoked. Miss Finch, who thought she knew all of his habits and moods, had never seen before that curious sort of a smile.

"Oh . . ." she said, wondering what in the world had happened to Mr. Drake.

"Get him on the 'phone for me, please, Miss Finch," Stephen said, "and make an appointment for to-morrow."

"Yes, sir." What had happened? Miss Finch's tidy brown head was filled with puzzled conjectures. Mr. Drake wasn't himself. He hadn't asked for her sister, who was ill, or noticed the rose in the bud vase on his desk or opened the window the customary two inches. "There's a telegram," she said.

Stephen lifted a paper weight. The telegram had been sliced open with the letters. "Leaving immediately," it said, "keep children should reach Philadelphia to-morrow much annoyed." It was signed

H. G. Fales. That, Stephen thought, was " Uncle Herbert." He had used exactly ten words.

" Make that appointment for Monday," he said to Miss Finch who sat with the telephone in her hand. " I'll be rather busy to-morrow."

Miss Finch had read the telegram. She wondered about the " children " and hoped Mr. Drake would explain. But he didn't explain. His manner was preoccupied. Several times, when he was dictating, she was obliged, by clearing her throat or repeating a sentence, to bring him back to the letters. And in the middle of the afternoon he said:

" Call my home, Miss Finch, and tell Thomas not to drive in for me to-day. I have some important errands. I'll go out on the train."

And then, although it was only three o'clock and there were urgent matters demanding his attention, Stephen walked out of the office!

Miss Finch was astonished. This was something which had not happened before. Mr. Drake always told her where he was going when he left during office hours and gave her telephone numbers in case he should be wanted. Her pad told her that he had a conference with Mr. Van Wyck at four o'clock. And there was the Arnold case, all at sixes and sevens.

Well, it wasn't her place to worry. She was too conscientious. Her sister often told her that. " What does it get you? " she asked. Miss Finch felt aggrieved and, consequently, reckless. She fastened the hood on her typewriter and took a novel from the lowest drawer of her desk. Then, although it was only three o'clock and there were many things to be done, she settled herself to read until the clock struck five.

Miss Finch's astonishment would have been greater if her thoughts could have followed Stephen. The " important errands " had to do with the toy department at Wanamaker's. It had occurred to him that Kit might find it dull being ill with nothing to amuse him. A picture puzzle, he thought. He had liked them immensely when he was about Kit's age.

There were puzzles in great variety. Stephen selected two. The young lady clerk, impressed by his well-cut clothes and a top coat made in London was amiable and anxious to please.

" How old is your little boy? " she asked.

Stephen felt embarrassed, but pleased, as well. Pretending to have a family gave him a certain sense of importance. Besides, he couldn't tell the young lady that they were runaway children and didn't belong to him.

" There's one eleven or twelve," he said, thinking, at once, of Jamie.

The young lady clerk smiled. " Fathers never remember exactly," she said.

It gave him a light-headed feeling to be thought the father of Barbara's children—the Barbara he had loved. He thought of asking her, " Just how

old is Jamie now?" The light-headed feeling increased. He suffered himself to be led to the sec-
tion devoted to trains which ran on tracks with
bridges and tunnels and tiny painted stations.

"Shall I send them?" asked the young lady
clerk, after half an hour of demonstrating the trains.

"I'll take them," Stephen answered.

"It will make a large package, I'm afraid."

"That's quite all right."

Stephen forgot, for the moment, his aversion to
lumpy bundles. The trains, he thought, would keep
Jamie out of mischief. They would set them up in
the schoolroom out of Aunt Edith's way. He smiled
a bit sheepishly at the clerk and opened a pin seal
wallet.

It was a very large package. Stephen would have
been embarrassed if he had not been thinking of
other things. He thought, as the elevator plunged
downward, that he couldn't take home presents for
the boys without remembering the girls. He found,
without much difficulty, a shell bracelet for Gay.
Barbara's gift required more time.

"Something for a child?" asked the black satin
goddess behind the counter.

Stephen considered the question. She had seemed
a child last night when he had carried her, asleep,
in his arms, up to bed. This morning she had
seemed older. It was hard to judge her by ordinary
standards. She changed so bewilderingly. A child?
A young lady? Barbara ——

" She's eighteen," he compromised.

That, at least, was definite—the certain fact of her age.

" These are the latest." The black satin goddess presented a glittering tray.

Stephen was not satisfied. The trinkets did not look like Barbara. He wanted to find something odd and exquisite. She was like that, he thought, —odd and exquisite and charming.

He found it, at last, a carnelian pendant set in filigreed gold on a slender golden chain.

" That's sort of quaint," said the black satin goddess, and patted back a yawn.

Quaint and charming. Barbara ——

As he waited for the package, a woman paused at the counter. She smelled faintly of lilacs. Stephen remembered Emily. He shifted his bundles and glanced at his watch. Good Lord! He hadn't a minute to lose.

The florist had no white lilacs. There wasn't time to try at another shop. The pale yellow roses would have to do. He added the florist's box to his accumulation of bundles, plunged out of the shop with undignified haste and hailed a passing taxi.

A family is distracting, he thought again, as he relaxed against the upholstery and lit a soothing cigarette. Well, it wasn't for long. The children's relatives were coming to-morrow. Kit couldn't be moved just yet, of course. But bronchitis wasn't serious. In a week or two . . .

III

The apartment near Rittenhouse Square was as restful and charming as usual. Emily rose from a chair beside the fire as the maid, crisply aproned, led Stephen into the living-room.

"Gracious!" she said brightly. "You look like Santa Claus, Stephen."

"Some things for the children."

"Oh. . . ." A little of the brightness slipped from Emily's face. The children!

The maid took the packages. Stephen spoke to Professor Trent, seated in an armchair beneath a lamp with an amber shade. He wore a black skull cap and a smoking jacket and a ponderous book lay open across his knees.

"Good-afternoon," the little professor said feeling rather uneasy. Emily had told him to excuse himself when Stephen came. But his chair was comfortable and he liked the warmth of the fire. He would just pretend that he hadn't heard.

"I owe you an apology." Stephen presented the florist's box. "I'll let these make it for me."

"They're lovely!" Emily breathed, lifting from the box the tangle of roses and fragile asparagus fern. Roses! she thought, feeling her spirits sink. She had hoped they would be lilacs. But he mustn't know she was disappointed. "A vase, Agnes," she said brightly. "The crystal one. Of course we understood." She deftly arranged the flowers. Didn't they look a little faded? "We missed you. But we understood, didn't we, Father-darling?"

"What's that?" The old man looked up owlishly. "Yes, yes," he said. "Of course we did, my dear." He dipped his chin into his collar and made himself as small as he could. Emily was "nervous" to-day. It wouldn't do to cross her. He hoped Stephen would stay for dinner. There were lamb chops when Stephen stayed, and salad and crisp little tarts. His mouth watered, thinking of the tarts. Usually, in the evening, they had toast and jam and tea.

Why didn't Father excuse himself? Emily wondered nervously. He was exasperating at times. But she smiled at Stephen and led him to a sofa a little removed from the fire. Father's hearing was dull. She hoped that Stephen knew.

"Tell me about the children," she said, folding her hands in her lap. "I must admit I'm curious. Who are they, Stephen?"

He told her, making an appealing story of the somewhat distressing facts. He thought Emily would understand. She seemed fond of children. She often told him about her "dear little friends" whom she met in the Square on sunny afternoons.

"You mean they actually ran away?" she asked when he had finished.

"Actually." Stephen did not look at Emily. The smile, half provoked, half amused touched the corners of his lips. "In a truck," he added, "at five o'clock in the morning."

"Poor Stephen!" Emily, gentle and understanding, lightly touched his hand. "We'll have to forgive them, I suppose. Children brought up as they have been ———"

"What do you mean?" Stephen asked, surprised at the note of resentment in his voice.

"Well, artists ———" she said vaguely.

Stephen checked the impulse to make a caustic comment. He had been rude to Emily last night. He must be gentle with her to-day. But, instead of telling her the things he had meant to say in the conservatory, he found himself talking about the children. It seemed necessary, somehow, to explain their reasons for running away. He realized, as he talked, that he was making a heroine of Barbara. But she *was* appealing. He was a bit surprised to find himself telling Emily about their talk last night in the library. He did not tell her, however, about carrying her up to bed.

"How old is she?" Emily asked.

"Eighteen." Why, he thought irritably, did everyone seem to think her age was so important?

"Oh," Emily said slowly. "Then she isn't a child."

"In some ways she seems younger than any of them." Stephen remembered the soft hair tumbling against her shoulders, her frank brown eyes, her childish faith in his ability to help her keep the children. "Kit is as grave as a judge. Gay is, I rather suspect, an artful little minx. Jamie seems to have a sort of sturdy independence. But Barbara ——"

This Barbara, Emily thought, was the artful minx and not Gay, who had seemed, when she met her last night, a pretty, polite little girl. Girls of eighteen, in this modern generation, seemed to know how to get what they wanted. She was afraid that Stephen was being taken in. These children! She wished they had stayed in Provincetown.

But she told Stephen none of her thoughts. She exerted herself to be gentle and understanding.

"Poor little darlings!" she said, and then, because she felt that she simply *must* know, "You aren't going to keep them?"

"Only for a week or two. Kit is ill. We'll have to keep him until he has recovered."

"Poor Stephen! It's very upsetting for you," Emily murmured softly.

"It can't be helped."

"You're very generous." Emily's lifted eyes shone with flattering admiration. "It's what I would have expected you to do."

"Dear . . ." Stephen pressed her hand, touched by the expression in her eyes. "I knew you would understand."

Emily's heart leapt and sank again. Stephen was glancing at his watch.

"I must go," he said and rose from the sofa.

"You couldn't have dinner with us?" Emily

stood beside him, wanting to keep him, her hand upon his sleeve.

The little professor, napping in the armchair, heard dimly the magic word " dinner."

" Yes, do," he said cordially, thinking of strawberry tarts.

" Thank you," Stephen said absently. " I can't manage it this evening. I'm a bit worried about the boy."

Emily's heart sank lower. Stephen, already, had left her, had left the room, pleasant in the light of the shaded lamps. He was thinking of the children, and Barbara. She called him back, silently. He did not seem to hear.

" Is there anything I can do? " she asked, annoyed at the flutter in her voice, unable to control it.

" Will you come to see them? " Stephen looked at her so tenderly that her heart leapt again. " I should like you to know them, Emily."

" I certainly will. Poor little darlings! " She felt quite fond of the children because Stephen wanted her to know them. She even felt fond of Barbara. She smiled at him, gently understanding.

But her spirits drooped again when he had gone. She looked at the yellow roses opening in the heat. They meant no more than an apology. Had Stephen forgotten those moments in the conservatory? He had said nothing definite. But she was sure he had meant —— If the children hadn't come when they

did —— Suddenly she couldn't bear the aching disappointment. Her lips trembled, her eyes filled with
tears. She went into her bedroom and quietly closed
the door.

The book, slipping from his knees to the floor,
roused the little professor. He yawned and looked
at the clock. The fire had died down and he was
hungry. Didn't Emily intend to have supper to-
night?

He started toward her bedroom, walking cau-
tiously, smelled the camphor she used when she had
a headache. Then, hearing footsteps, he scurried
back to the armchair. Emily was a devoted daughter. But she had been "nervous" all day. It
wouldn't do to cross her. He dipped his chin into
his collar and made himself very small.

But it wasn't Emily. It was Agnes, no longer
crisply aproned, her feet in shapeless felt slippers
with bedraggled magenta bows. She shuffled in
with a tray.

"You might as well eat here," she said, setting
the tray on his knees. "Miss Trent's not feeling
well. She don't want any supper."

The little professor looked at the tray. Toast
and jam and very weak tea. He thought of lamb
chops and strawberry tarts. He wished that
Stephen had stayed.

CHAPTER IV

I

THE telegram had inadequately expressed Uncle Herbert's state of mind. He was very angry, indeed. It would have taken more than ten words, Stephen thought, when Uncle Herbert exploded in the office. He was glad he had sent them the office address. The children would be spared the worst of the explosion. Certainly Uncle Herbert couldn't continue to rant indefinitely. There weren't enough words in the English language to supply him with ammunition.

Aunt Lola, who had come with Uncle Herbert to represent the relatives, wasn't angry. She was merely very much hurt. It was Barbara's fault, she repeated, whenever Uncle Herbert paused to catch a breath. Dear little Gay would never have thought of such a thing. Barbara, she feared, was like her mother, wilful and headstrong, with no proper regard for other people's feelings. Oh dear, it was all very confusing and sad!

"Barbara is an unusual child," Stephen said, nettled by Aunt Lola's remarks.

"Wilful and headstrong," the plump little lady repeated, smoothing the folds of her moleskin wrap.

"Impulsive, perhaps." Stephen controlled, with difficulty, his growing irritation. "But not headstrong. She is, I think, too reasonable for her age."

"Reasonable!" Uncle Herbert's face was very red. "Was it reasonable to run away?"

"It was not very wise," Stephen said. "But you understand her motive. She wanted to keep the children together."

"A notion! All a notion!" Uncle Herbert stormed.

"We can't blame her too much, I suppose," Aunt Lola said with a fluttering sigh. "It's the way she has been brought up. Christopher Thorne was ——" Respect for the dead caused Aunt Lola to pause. But her expression implied many things. "Poor Barbara!" She sighed again. "I'm afraid she hadn't a happy life."

Stephen had thought her the happiest person he had ever known—the Barbara he had loved. "I'm the black sheep of the family," she had told him a very long time ago. "They think I'm a little crazy. I am," she had said with an enchanting smile. "I'm crazy about my Kit. . . ."

Through Uncle Herbert's voice, he heard her voice, gay and amused; through Aunt Lola's perfume, which was making his head ache a little, he smelled the roses of southern France. It seemed an act of treachery to Barbara to deliver her children into the hands of the enemy. But what in the world could he do?

"They have put us in a humiliating position," Uncle Herbert was saying when Stephen's attention returned to the office. "We are willing to do our duty toward Barbara's children. But they don't know the meaning of gratitude."

That, Stephen thought, was the true reason for Uncle Herbert's rage. His pride had been wounded. He couldn't feel that any of these relatives were deeply attached to the children. They wanted the satisfaction of doing an unpleasant duty. Some people were like that, he thought. Doing an unpleasant duty inflated their self-esteem. Duty, he thought, was a poor substitute for sympathy and love and understanding.

The younger Barbara had made him see them so clearly, these relatives who meant to be kind but couldn't understand. He knew how Kit felt about Uncle Herbert who talked a great deal of duty and gratitude but did not mention affection. And he suspected that Aunt Lola, with her massaged-looking skin and her hair a shade too golden, was, as Barbara had reported, rather " a silly woman." His heart warmed toward the children. He found himself wanting to protect them. It gave him a queer sort of feeling.

"Kit is a bit ill," he said when Uncle Herbert's rage had subsided a little and Aunt Lola had ceased to sigh. "We'll have to keep him a week or two."

Uncle Herbert's expression indicated that this was the final indignity.

"I must get back to the office," he said, louder than was necessary. "I have wasted a great deal of time."

"There's no reason for you to stay." Stephen felt that his patience was fraying at the edges. "We'll send Kit to you as soon as he is well enough to travel."

"What about Jamie?" Aunt Lola asked.

"Barbara can take him to Maine, I suppose. Unless," Uncle Herbert added grimly humorous, "she takes a notion to start for China instead."

"Aunt Josephine is very much annoyed." Aunt Lola thought of the irate old lady in the red brick Providence house.

Stephen thought of her, too,—as Barbara had described her. He felt again a disturbing desire to guard and protect the children. He knew it was an unreasonable desire. Aunt Josephine, no doubt, was a very estimable old lady. But it seemed a shame that Barbara should be forced to live where she had once been so unhappy. He was reluctant to send her to Providence. Stephen, of course, knew nothing at all about Bruce.

"I can take Gay at once, I suppose?" Aunt Lola asked. "There are such delightful children at the hotel. I'm sure she will have a lovely time."

Hotel children! Stephen thought with a silent groan. He had seen them in many places; pert

over-dressed little girls, little boys who bullied the
porters and maids and smoked cigarettes on the sly.
Gay hadn't Barbara's character. Looking at Aunt
Lola, it was easy to see what pretty Gay would probably become. Still, there was no reason why he
should make himself responsible. He was sorry for
the four Thornes. But what in the world could he
do?

"I suppose so," he said with no great enthusiasm.
Gay, he thought, would be entirely willing to go with
Aunt Lola.

But Gay surprised him, when they reached
Stephen's home that afternoon.

"Oh no, Aunt Lola," she said, her warm color
deepening. "I couldn't leave Kit when he's sick."

She sat on the side of the huge bed helping Kit fit
together one of the picture puzzles. Barbara sat
in the stuffed damask chair, with an open book on
her knees. She had been reading aloud to Jamie
when Stephen brought Aunt Lola and Uncle Herbert into the room. The reading had stopped
abruptly and the color had paled from her cheeks.
A little of it returned when Gay said, sweetly but
firmly:

"Oh no, Aunt Lola. I can't leave Kit when he's
sick."

"But we mustn't impose on Mr. Drake." Aunt
Lola was hurt by Gay's lack of interest in the trip
to Florida. "The dear little thing adores me," she
often told her friends.

"Are we imposing?" Gay asked, glancing up at Stephen from under her long curled lashes.

They all looked at Stephen, Barbara, Kit, Gay and Jamie. He felt that he couldn't fail them.

"It's pleasant having you here," he said and realized, with a start of surprise, that what he said was true.

Four pairs of eyes rewarded him. Four faces, which had looked very anxious a moment ago, broke into sudden smiles.

"Thank you," Kit croaked.

"Thank you," said Jamie's smile and Barbara's and Gay's.

Aunt Lola was plaintive but Gay was firm. She couldn't leave Kit when he was sick. If Uncle Stephen didn't mind, she would very much rather stay. "Uncle Stephen" didn't mind. It was decided that Gay should go to Florida later.

"There is always someone going that way," Stephen said. "The Newbolds will take her, perhaps."

"The Mercer Newbolds?" Aunt Lola asked.

"They are old friends of ours."

Aunt Lola was pleased and excited. Dear George had left her some money. There was the dove-gray car and the chauffeur named Pierre. But Dear George had, unfortunately, left her no social standing worthy of the name. She fancied herself telling ladies on the veranda of the Florida hotel, "My niece will join me later. She is coming with the

Newbolds—the Mercer Newbolds from German-
town." The fancy charmed Aunt Lola. She was
almost grateful to Barbara for running away with
the children.

Uncle Herbert was almost grateful, too,—but for
another reason. It was just as well, he thought, that
Kit should be ill here. Emma had her hands full.
It would save her a great deal of extra work.

Uncle Herbert behaved very well. An excellent
luncheon had mellowed his temper. A glass of
sherry, in the library downstairs, had greatly assisted the luncheon. He scolded the children for
running away in a somewhat jocular fashion. He
asked Kit riddles and tousled Gay's curls and admired Jamie's electric trains. He was agreeable to
Barbara. He produced a check-book and pen.

"That's quite all right," Stephen said.

"But there must be expenses." Uncle Herbert,
looking important, unscrewed the top from the pen.

"Let me take care of them please."

"Couldn't think of it, Mr. Drake." Uncle Herbert was pompous and dignified. Drake, he thought,
could afford it, of course. But the family pride was
at stake.

"I'd rather. They are my guests." Stephen
looked at Barbara whose cheeks were flushed with
embarrassment. "I have some claim on them, you
know," he added with a smile. "Barbara is my
little fillette."

"My little fillette!" . . . Barbara felt a

singing inside of herself. Uncle Stephen, she thought, was the kindest man in the world.

"If you insist ——" Uncle Herbert said doubt-fully.

"I certainly do."

"Well, well ——" The check-book was restored to Uncle Herbert's pocket. He looked kindly at the children. "We can't expect old heads on young shoulders, I suppose," he said to Stephen and ac-cepted another cigar.

They left some time later, declining an invitation to dinner. Uncle Herbert was going back to Pitts-burgh. Aunt Lola thought she would drive on to Washington where her daughter, Gwen, was visiting friends. They were extremely grateful to Mr. Drake. They kissed the children "Good-bye" and left behind a very great deal of advice.

The children greeted him jubilantly when Stephen returned to the room where Kit lay, propped against pillows, after Aunt Lola and Uncle Herbert had gone and he had given Aunt Edith, transplanting ferns in the conservatory, a sketchy account of the interview.

"What did you do to them?" Barbara asked. "They were so very polite."

"I conjured them," Stephen said, relaxing in an easy chair after what had been a very trying day.

"Really conjured them, Uncle Stephen?" Jamie hung over the back of the chair. His eyes were wide with interest.

"You must have," Barbara said, her eyes bright with relief. "I thought Uncle Herbert would simply explode."

"He did," Stephen said and the smile, half amused, half provoked, touched the corners of his lips.

"Was it very dreadful?" Barbara asked anxiously.

"Pretty bad," Stephen said.

"Poor Uncle Stephen!" Gay, perched on the arm of the chair, laid her glowing cheek against Stephen's.

"I guess Uncle Stephen could manage them," Jamie said admiringly, spilling himself over the back of the chair. "He's a pretty smart lawyer, I guess."

"Did you mean it?" Barbara asked shyly.

"Mean what?" Stephen looked up at the vivid face framed in tendrils of soft brown hair.

"That it was pleasant having us here."

"Of course I did." Again Stephen realized that what he said was true.

Jamie and Gay fell upon him with rapturous cries. Stephen felt himself half smothered in thin young arms and lusty bear-like embraces. It did something strange to his heart. His arms, which were not accustomed to children, tightened strongly about them. He looked over their heads at Barbara standing beside Kit's bed. Her eyes thanked him. She smiled her gayest smile. Bless them, he thought, with a

lump in his throat.   What jolly youngsters they
were!

They sang to celebrate a victory.

> *"We sail the ocean blue*
> *We catch-a da plenty-a fish.*
> *The wind she blow like hell.*
> *The rain come down my whiskers . . ."*

They sang lustily to tell Uncle Stephen how very
happy they were.   "Chips" set up an unmusical
barking.   Kit croaked a line or two from the huge
carved bed and tinkled an accompaniment with a
spoon on his medicine glass—

> *"Merry-o, my good companions*
> *Viva la Garibaldi*
> *Viva!   Viva!*
> *Viva l'Italia!"*

Aunt Edith opened the door, her face beneath
waved white hair very stern and disapproving.

"The doctor advised rest and quiet," she said
when she could be heard.

"A little pleasant excitement won't hurt him."
Stephen smiled at Kit, propped against the pillows.
It did not occur to him that he might look undignified with the children swarming over him and his
tie disarranged and his hair mussed.   "We're cele-
brating," he said.   "The enemy has been routed."

"Whoopee!" Jamie shouted, his freckled face
shining with happy excitement.

They swung into the chorus again. " Chips "
barked more shrilly than ever. Jamie, to Aunt
Edith's horror, beat time with a pair of drumsticks
that used to be Stephen's against the foot of the
bed. Kit tinkled the spoon against the glass and
croaked like a happy bullfrog.

> *" We sail the ocean blue*
> *We catch-a da plenty-a fish.*
> *The wind she blow like hell.*
> *The rain come down my whiskers."*

" Gracious! " Aunt Edith thought and buttoned
her lips together.

II

That evening Barbara wrote to Bruce—

> . . . Kit is sick, but not very, just
> a cold and a temperature. I was worried
> but Kit says it's " an act of Providence "—
> you know the old-fashioned way he talks.
> Anyhow, Uncle Stephen will let us stay
> here until Kit is better, although he was
> provoked about us running away. I think
> he's getting to like us a little. He brought
> us presents last night—a lovely necklace
> for me—and he has been so kind about
> Kit.
>
> Aunt Lola and Uncle Herbert came to-
> day but they were very polite. I think

they were impressed by Uncle Stephen's home. It's very elegant, Bruce. The name of it is " Thornhedge " because of a prickly hedge that came from England or somewhere, and it's built out of stone with ivy all over it and stables (only they don't have horses now) and greenhouses and lawns and gardens and lovely trees. And a butler!!! What do you think of that? It's a very educating experience to live in a house that has a name and a butler and cords with tassels to ring for the servants. There are six of them, Henry and Sarah, Henry's wife, and Bessie who is very deaf and Martin, the chauffeur, Katie, and the gardener whose name is Alfred. They are all lovely to us, especially Henry. I think Sarah henpecks him. He has a ' meaching ' look whenever she's around.

There is a library just full of books and a drawing-room all full of rosewood furniture and chandeliers with glass icicles dripping from them and cabinets full of the loveliest things; little jade trees and ivory elephants and flowers made out of glass. And a conservatory!!! I didn't know people had conservatories and drawing-rooms except in books, did you, Bruce darling? But, of course, this is a very old house. Uncle Stephen's grandfather had it built simply ages ago and some of the furniture looks as though it should be in a museum, sort of heavy and carved, you know, with faded looking upholstery and fringe and tassels and things.

We have a great deal to live up to because, although Mother's relatives are "well to do," they don't live in places like this. Gay is simply entranced! You know how she loves elegance! But I wish we were back in Provincetown with Martha scolding us and Manuel playing his accordion and Father coming in from the studio with paint on his trousers and his hair all mussed up, making jokes and telling us stories the way he used to do. Uncle Stephen tells stories. But they aren't like Father's. Father was a very amusing parent, no matter what anyone says.

I miss Father so much. And I miss you, too. I'm dreadfully homesick at night. Gay and I sleep in an enormous room with a canopy over the bed and four full length mirrors and a gray carpet covered all over with roses. And we have a bathroom of our own!!!

But I do get homesick, thinking of you, because " home " doesn't mean Provincetown or any special place but just wherever you are. I put myself to sleep every night by telling myself a story. I did in Provincetown after Father died. Do you know what the story is, Bruce? It's the one about the silver flute. If I keep very still I imagine I can hear it. Is that silly and sentimental? I suppose it is but I'm that way. If ever the flute stopped playing, I should simply want to die. Don't let it stop playing its one lovely song . . . "I love you, pretty gypsy girl with the roses in your hair. . . ."

Do you see this blot on the paper? That's a tear. . . .

I couldn't help it. I want to see you so much. Wouldn't it be wonderful if Uncle Stephen would keep the children and I could come to New York? I know they'd be safe and happy here. He's so lovely and kind.

But I don't suppose he will. His Aunt Edith doesn't like us. She's sort of stout and stiff, if you know what I mean. She wishes we hadn't come. But it's Uncle Stephen's house so she doesn't say anything, but I know she'd like to, just the same. She swells up like a hop-toad and her face gets pink and she closes her mouth in a funny tight way. I haven't a nice disposition, have I, Bruce? But what

can you expect of a " gypsy girl "? I don't
suppose they ever have any manners.

There's another blot! I do love you so
much. But I haven't told Uncle Stephen.
He might think it was ridiculous because
I am only eighteen. It's a beautiful secret
and no one knows it but you and me, and
the ring with the little gold heart. Here's
all my love, except what belongs to the
children, tied up in paper covered with
stars with a huge silver bow. It makes a
very large package. Keep it, Bruce, from

Your Babbie,
who loves you very much.

P. S. I asked Uncle Stephen to call me
Babbie instead of Barbara. He does.
He's very accommodating.

P. S. No. 2. He isn't a " crusty old
bachelor." He's nice looking. But old. I
guess he must be forty.

P. S. No. 3. Here's a kiss for good-
night. Know something? I love you.

CHAPTER V

I

KIT gradually improved. He sat in the school-room, now, in an armchair filled with pillows with an afghan over his knees. Stephen brought him a table which fitted across the arms of the chair and Kit was busy all day with his drawing pencils and water colors and the books Barbara selected from the library shelves downstairs.

The schoolroom became the center of the house. There was always a fire in the open grate and cheerful red curtains shut out the dreariness of the late November days. Jamie's electric trains were set up on the floor. Gay played games with Kit, or Barbara, curled on a shabby red sofa with comfortable curves and hollows, read aloud to the children. Katie, the cook, sent Henry up with cookies baked into star and crescent shapes and sprinkled over with sugar. Alfred, the gardener, came up to show Kit a small potted apple tree or a cactus plant which reminded them all of stories of the desert. Aunt Edith, also, paid an occasional visit to the schoolroom. But the children, with the exception of Gay, were somewhat constrained with her. They knew Aunt Edith wished that they hadn't come.

Stephen went to the schoolroom, first, when he returned home in the evening. He was always greeted with rapturous cries and lusty embraces. He looked forward, each day, to the hour before dinner which he spent with the four Thornes. They told him things which had happened during the day. Kit would have a sketch to show him, perhaps. Jamie would have found a family of kittens in the old sleigh in the stable. Gay would want to dress up for him in a hoop-skirt and flowered bonnet she had discovered in the attic. Barbara would ask his advice about Jamie's cut finger or Kit's appetite which wasn't what it should be. And didn't he think that Gay should learn to spell ten new words every day?

There were arguments for him to settle.

" How can the sun come up like thunder? " Gay asked one evening and Stephen knew they had been reading Kipling.

" I suppose it means suddenly," Stephen said when he had thought a little. The children's questions sometimes embarrassed him. They expected him to know everything, " because he was a lawyer."

" Does it make a noise? " Jamie asked. " A loud noise like thunder? "

" Not actually, I suppose."

" But China isn't right across a bay from Manda-

lay," Kit said with the air of an experienced travel-
ler who had first hand information about flying fishes
and palm trees and temple bells.

"But it must be, Kit." Barbara joined the dis-
cussion.

"It isn't."

"It must be or Kipling ———"

"Is it, Uncle Stephen?"

Stephen sent Jamie down to the library for an
atlas, and the argument became a geography lesson
conducted by Kit.

The four Thornes argued about anything; modern painting, pirates, what made seeds grow when
they were planted, why the kangaroo had two short
legs in front. They had been encouraged, Stephen
thought, whatever the limitations of their training,
to exercise their minds.

"Aunt Josephine calls arguing 'talking back,'"
Barbara said one evening. "But it isn't, is it, Uncle
Stephen?"

"Of course it isn't," Stephen said. "Everyone
has a right to his own opinions."

"Even children," Kit said thoughtfully. "Father always liked us to have our own opinions."

Stephen liked it, too. He found the Thornes, as
they became rested and more accustomed to their
surroundings, increasingly entertaining. He was
pleased, and a little flattered as well, because they
accepted him on intimate terms. They were never
reserved and polite with him as they were with Aunt

Edith. It gave him the feeling of having shed a number of dreary years.

Barbara delighted him especially. She was such a bewildering combination of rather precocious wisdom and childish simplicity. She had no airs or poses, it was impossible to judge her by ordinary standards. Sometimes when she romped with the children, cheeks flushed, brown curls tumbling, she seemed the youngest of them all and, sometimes, her manner was quaintly grown up and her eyes were too big for her face. But the unhappy times never lasted long. Barbara's spirits were elastic. She was odd and exquisite and unaccountable. She had the gift of laughter.

It was pleasant to do things for her, to see her eyes brighten with pleasure, to hear the singing notes in her gay young voice.

"You'll spoil her, Stephen," Aunt Edith said when he continued to bring her odd little gifts.

"She can stand it, I think," Stephen replied. "I want her to be happy while she is here."

And then he forgot Aunt Edith. Barbara was coming downstairs to meet him, looking small and demure and very pretty in a bodiced frock the color of a primrose.

"Did you have a hard day at the office?" she asked, smiling up at him with the disturbing dimple at the corner of her mouth. "Come up and put on your slippers and let me light your pipe."

Of course she was only a child, Aunt Edith told

herself. But Stephen was certainly bewitched. She thought kindly of Emily as she watched Stephen and Barbara walk upstairs, her gay young laugh drifting back to Aunt Edith. Stephen shouldn't be allowed to make a fool of himself. Not if she could help it. Aunt Edith shook her head and buttoned her lips together.

Stephen took the girls on a shopping expedition. It was Natalie who put the idea into his head.

"They're pretty," she said, having tea with Stephen after a visit to the schoolroom. "It would be fun to dress them properly."

"Aren't they properly dressed?" Stephen asked, smiling with pleasure because Natalie thought his guests were attractive.

Natalie thought more than that. She thought that the children were good for Stephen, in spite of the fuss Aunt Edith made. He seemed younger and more—well, human. She and Bob had agreed that Stephen needed to be jolted out of his comfortable rut.

But she did not put her thoughts into words. She stirred her tea with a thin silver spoon and smiled at Stephen through the firelight.

"Men don't notice such things, I suppose. But little girls like pretty clothes. Will you let me take them shopping?"

Stephen agreed, in an absent-minded fashion, and presently changed the subject. But he did not forget what Natalie had said.

"Barbara," he said that evening, finding her alone in the library after the children had gone to bed, "wouldn't you like to go shopping?"

"Shopping for what?" she asked, closing the book she had been reading.

"I thought you or Gay might need something," Stephen said vaguely. "Dresses, slippers—something like that."

"I'm afraid we can't, Uncle Stephen."

"Why not?"

She flushed and looked down at the book.

"I—we haven't any money."

Stephen saw the flush. He knew that he had blundered.

"I'd like to buy them for you," he said.

Her lashes lifted. She looked at him gravely.

"Oh, no," she said quickly. "Thank you very much. But we—I—can't let you do that."

"Why not?"

"How could we ever pay you back?"

"Must you?" Stephen asked, liking her independence, wondering how he could buy her the clothes she needed without hurting her pride.

"Of course," she said, as though there could be no question at all about that. "But we are shabby, aren't we?" Her fingers touched the worn frock. "I don't want you to be ashamed of us."

"I'm not," Stephen said quickly, watching the pucker, soft as a wrinkle in silk, between her curving brows.

"You have reason to be," she decided, after an interval of thought. "Maybe we could pay you back. There'll be some money when they sell the Provincetown house."

"That's a good idea," Stephen agreed. "I'll present you with all of the bills."

"Promise?" she asked very gravely.

"I promise," he gravely agreed.

A day or two later he took them shopping, leaving the office at noon with no explanations, which caused Miss Finch, a blue serge bundle of questions, to wonder more than ever what had happened to Mr. Drake.

Stephen wondered, too. The children, he thought, were discovering for him qualities which he did not know that he possessed. He was suddenly interested in hats and dresses and slippers. That was the reason he gave himself, as he walked down Chestnut Street with Barbara and Gay. But there was a deeper reason involved. He jealously wanted to do everything for Barbara's children himself as long as they were with him. He couldn't share them with Natalie. He did it for her—the Barbara he had loved.

He was a little embarrassed, at first, by the suave salesladies in the shop Natalie had recommended. It was a new experience. He had never bought clothes for girls. But the embarrassment gradually merged into interest and pride. Gay was enchanting in the frocks which the salesladies selected.

"Sweet!" they murmured to each other, loud enough for Stephen to hear. "A real little beauty!"

Gay wore her look of a little girl who had just given her shoes to an orphan. But Stephen knew she had heard the admiring comments. She was an artful little minx but she was also a beauty. It embarrassed and pleased him, too, when she flung her arms around his neck and cried happily:

"Oh, Uncle Stephen, aren't they perfectly sweet!"

"We can't afford much for me," Barbara said when they had selected frocks for Gay and a coat with a squirrel collar and a cap banded with soft, dark fur.

"Try them on anyway," Stephen suggested, seeing the wistful expression in her eyes.

They changed her amazingly, he thought. He had not realized the magic of pretty clothes. He had thought her attractive in the Provincetown jerseys and pleated skirts, in the shabby velveteen dress. In these longer frocks, cunningly cut and fitted, she looked older—until he saw her eyes. Then she looked like a little girl dressing up.

"We can't," she protested when Stephen would have instructed the saleslady to send the enchanting frocks.

"One or two?" He smiled at her.

"One or two," she agreed, quickly returning the smile.

The saleslady displayed a short fur jacket the color of coffee with cream.

"Gracious!" Barbara exclaimed. "I can't buy fur coats, Uncle Stephen!"

"Try it on," he suggested.

She slipped her arms into the coat.

"Isn't it sweet?" the saleslady asked.

"Perfectly lovely!" breathed Gay.

"Will you let me buy it for a present?" Stephen asked when the saleslady had disappeared in quest of other temptations. She looked charming in the jacket and the soft little pull on hat.

"I can't, Uncle Stephen," she said. "You've done so much for us. I can't let you buy presents like this."

"Barbara," Stephen said, "do you know what a godfather is?"

"An act of Providence," Gay said brightly, "at least that's what Kit says."

"He's a second father," Stephen said. "Now, will you let me buy you the coat?"

"But you've done so much, Uncle Stephen."

"I like doing things for you," Stephen said gently. "It gives me a great deal of pleasure."

"Then I'd let him," Gay advised.

Barbara finally agreed.

"Thank you," she said, when they had decided that she should wear the coat. "I guess I have a frivolous disposition. I wish ——" She paused and a wistful expression crept into her eyes. She wished Bruce could see her in the fur jacket with the muff and the soft little pull on hat. They were becoming. She did look very nice.

Stephen saw the wistful expression. He thought she wished that her father might see her. Or her mother, perhaps. Stephen, of course, knew nothing at all about Bruce.

That evening Barbara saw, for the first time, the painting which hung above the fireplace in Stephen's room.

"I wanted you to see me," she said, standing in the open door just before time for dinner. She wore one of the frocks they had selected that afternoon, a frock the color of a tea-rose, which fell to her ankles in graceful folds. There were heels on her buckled bronze slippers and she had pinned in her curls at the nape of her neck.

"You look very nice," Stephen said, feeling a strange disturbance in his heart.

And then she saw the painting; red rocks, blue sea, distant rust-colored sails, a girl with the wind blowing her skirt against her bare brown legs.

"Father did that!" she said, moving toward the fireplace.

"Yes," Stephen said.

"It's Mother." She stood looking up at the painting, her lashes misted with tears. "It isn't Mother's face exactly but the rest of it is."

"Yes," Stephen said again.

"She was lovely, wasn't she?"

"Very lovely." Was it memories of the Barbara
he had loved, Stephen wondered, or was it the Barbara in the tea-rose frock that caused the strange disturbance in his heart? He saw her, standing there
in the firelight, as he had not seen her before. She
seemed, for a moment, a woman old enough to be
loved as he had loved her mother.

II

Emily came to see Barbara and the children.

The visit was not entirely a success. She came one
rainy Saturday afternoon and Henry took her directly up to the schoolroom. Stephen was there
with the children. There was a fire in the grate and
the lamps were lighted and the red curtains were
drawn against the rainy world outside.

The room was in an uproar. They had been playing some sort of a noisy game. It seemed to Emily,
nervous about the visit, that there must be a great
many more than three children and one small yellow
dog. All of this, she thought, must be very upsetting to Stephen who liked quiet and order. Certainly there was neither quiet nor order in the room
with the drawn red curtains.

Stephen did not appear to be upset. He came to
meet her, smiling, drew her into the room.

"You're just in time," he said. "We're playing
a very exciting game."

He had wanted Emily to see the children. He

had thought that she would be friendly and gracious. She was—but with a difference. Her manner was playful and slightly condescending. She made the fatal error of calling them " Stephen's kiddies."

" Will you let me play the game with you? " she asked, smiling a shade too brightly, Stephen thought. They weren't babies, these children of his. They were intelligent. Why must Emily use that patronizing tone?

The children lost interest in the game. They were reserved and very polite. It was apparent that they did not intend to include Emily in the happy intimacy which Stephen shared. Conversation, which had been gay and spontaneous, became painfully labored. Stephen had wanted Emily to see the children at their best. They could be very appealing. Now they looked like bored little puppets whose strings weren't working well.

Barbara joined them, presently. She wore Kit's belted trench coat and her hair, under a brown beret, was curled into ringlets by the rain.

" This is Barbara," Stephen said, thinking how pretty she looked.

" How do you do, Miss Trent," Barbara said, poised and self-possessed. " I'm rather drippy, I'm afraid. I've been walking in the rain."

She wasn't a child, Emily thought, resenting Barbara's poise, resenting her glowing cheeks and the curly soft brown hair. Her manner was gracious and reserved. She was a very pretty girl.

Conversation became increasingly difficult.

"Are you having a nice visit?" Emily asked.

"Very nice," Barbara answered, removing the coat and the brown beret.

"Very nice," Gay echoed, trying to be tactful and polite.

"I found some kittens in a sleigh," Jamie ventured, making conversation.

"*Did* you?" Emily asked too brightly.

"Chips" advanced, baring his teeth in what Jamie called "a smile." Emily drew herself into the depths of the chair. She was timid about strange dogs.

"Here, 'Chips'!" Jamie called, withering scorn in his voice. Couldn't this lady see that "Chips" was smiling and wanting to be friendly? He wished she would leave so they could go on with the game.

Emily had brought Kit a book—"The Motorboat Boys in Southern Waters." Kit thanked her politely and laid it aside. Emily felt that something was wrong. And then she noticed that "Moby Dick" lay on the table beside Kit's chair. The book she had brought was too juvenile, though the clerk in the book-shop had assured her that it was a favorite with boys of any age. She grew pink with confusion. She wished that she had not come.

She wanted to be charming to the children. All the way out she had pictured herself winning their immediate affection. But everything was wrong. She introduced subjects which she thought might interest them. They were polite but bored. Emily became increasingly nervous. Her head ached. She felt as though she were getting a cold.

If only she wouldn't try so hard, Stephen thought, feeling sorry for Emily, resenting her inability to interest the children. If she would treat them as equals instead of using that playful tone. He exerted himself to restore the usual gayety of the schoolroom. It was useless. Emily was nervous and uneasy. Barbara looked uncomfortable. The children were bored and polite.

There was, however, one bright moment amid the difficulties of the visit. Gay, a born diplomat, admired Emily's hair.

"It must look lovely when it's let down," she said, glancing up at Emily from under her long curled lashes. "Like the fairy tale—'Rapunzel, Rapunzel, let down your hair.'"

Emily flushed with pleasure. She hoped Stephen saw her as a fairy-tale princess. She relaxed, for a moment, and was friendly and gracious, especially to Gay.

But only for a moment. She saw Stephen look at Barbara, curled on the sofa in a smart little frock of honey-colored wool. She saw herself in the glass doors of the bookcase. She didn't look like a fairy-tale princess. She looked almost middle-aged, compared with Barbara's glowing youth. Her head throbbed painfully. She wished again that she hadn't come.

Henry brought tea and little frosted cakes. Barbara served it prettily.

" I've had lots of experience," she said to Emily, wanting to be friendly. " Father had ' Visiting Days ' at the studio. There were always a great many ladies. Father was very handsome."

" That must have been nice," Emily said vaguely. Stephen had said that Barbara was a child, " younger than any of them in many ways." She didn't act like a child. Her manner was assured. And the way she had been brought up ! Artists—

" Two lumps for you, Uncle Stephen." Barbara dimpled and smiled as she handed him the cup. " I've learned that, anyway."

Artful, Emily thought. Stephen looked at her so tenderly. But he looked at Emily, too. She felt better when they left the schoolroom and walked downstairs together. It was easier to think kindly of the children when they weren't embarrassing her by being bored and polite. She spoke of Gay with enthusiasm as they waited in the hall for Thomas to bring the car.

She knows I think less of Gay than any of them, Stephen thought. She's jealous of Barbara. That was absurd. Emily was too intelligent to be jealous of a child. He silently apologized. Stephen, as Aunt Edith had once before observed, had much to learn about women.

" Will you come for dinner some evening soon ? " Emily asked as Stephen settled her into the car and folded the robe about her. "Father enjoys your visits so much. You have rather neglected us lately."

Had he hesitated a moment too long before he had accepted the invitation, Emily wondered, as the car followed the winding drive. She told herself that Stephen had not changed. He must, of course, spend some time with the children. Everything would be right again when they had gone.

But her arguments were not convincing. Stephen *had* changed. Tears filled her eyes, spilled down over her cheeks. She hastily wiped them away, fearing that Thomas might turn around and see.

When Stephen returned to the schoolroom, he found the children engaged in a heated argument. They stopped talking, when he opened the door, and looked a little guilty.

"What's the matter?" he asked.

"Gay says you're goin' to marry her," Jamie said indignantly, his face and his ears very red.

"Jamie!" Barbara said.

"Shut up!" hissed Kit.

"Are you, Uncle Stephen?" asked Gay, who loved a romance.

"Why?" Stephen felt embarrassed. He lit a cigarette.

"Well," Gay reported, ignoring warning glances from Kit and Barbara, "Sarah told Henry you were and your Aunt Edith told Mrs. King. It seems as though everybody knows."

Did they? Stephen wondered irritably. He looked at Barbara, recalling what Aunt Edith had said a day or two ago. "You shouldn't pay so much attention to Barbara," Aunt Edith had said. "Girls are always ready to fall in love. You don't want to hurt her, Stephen."

Aunt Edith had "notions," Stephen thought. He had told her that a day or two ago. "She thinks I'm a nice old man," he had told Aunt Edith, annoyed at the fantastic notion that Barbara might fall in love with him. Annoyed, he remembered, but a little pleased, as well. It was flattering to think that the child found him attractive. But he hadn't thought, for a moment, that Aunt Edith had reasonable grounds for so fantastic a notion.

He was sure of it now. Barbara smiled at him from the sofa.

"Why shouldn't Uncle Stephen marry anyone he likes?" she asked with a merry disarming laugh. "He should have some children of his own. He knows how to treat them so nicely."

Stephen should have felt relieved. But, somehow, he didn't exactly.

III

Barbara wrote to Bruce—

    . . . We are to stay for Christmas. Isn't that lovely of Uncle Stephen? Kit

is lots better. Thomas took him for a
ride this afternoon and he's able, now, to
have meals in the dining-room. Dinner is
always like a party with flowers and candles and interesting things to eat. Aunt
Edith (I don't call her that to her face.
It would be too much like calling the
Queen of Belgium "Aunt Lizzie.") wishes
we'd have our meals in the schoolroom.
We do talk a lot, I guess, and sometimes
Jamie spills things. But Uncle Stephen
doesn't mind. He says he has just found
out that dinner can be an entertaining
occasion.

He's lovely, Bruce. He's teaching me
to ride a horse. I have a riding habit and
pull-on boots and a three-cornered hat that
is very " chic." (At least, that's what the
saleslady called it. Anyway, it's becoming.) Did you ever ride a horse? It's
thrilling and I haven't been stiff in my
joints since the first time. That is, not
very stiff.

Uncle Stephen took me to the opera the
other night all alone. The Opera!
Doesn't that sound grand? We sat in a
box, if you please, and I had a dress the
color of strawberries and cream and a
strawberry velvet wrap and gilt slippers
with buckles. I felt very elegant and not

at all like me. And the music, Bruce! It was " Madame Butterfly." I cried at the part where she waited all night for her lover and Uncle Stephen had to lend me his handkerchief because, with all my elegance, I hadn't remembered to bring one, which shows you that I haven't changed at all, in spite of sitting in a box at the opera and having a new dress. . . .

Bruce wrote to Barbara—

. . . It all sounds very exciting. I know you were lovely in the dress that looks like " strawberries and cream " but I'd rather think of you in a yellow jersey with a rip sewed up and an old brown skirt and sandals and socks. The dress like cream and strawberries would be too elegant for my studio which is up four flights of dingy stairs with a fruit store underneath.

I'm glad, of course, that you and the children will be together for Christmas. I had hoped that you would be here, though we'd probably be obliged to eat Christmas dinner at Child's. I'm trying to be patient. Don't fall in love with " Uncle Stephen," no matter how nice he is. . . .

Barbara answered—

That wasn't a nice letter, Bruce. It didn't sound a bit like you. Don't you know that I'd rather live up over the fruit store with you than anything else in the world? But Uncle Stephen has been so kind. I think he enjoys doing things for us. It's only being grateful to let him, isn't it? Besides, he *is* my godfather and that makes it all right.

I do love him in a way, of course. But not the way you mean. That's the way I love you. I told you Uncle Stephen is *old*. Forty, anyway, though he isn't bald and is very distinguished looking. But as for falling in love with him—Bruce MacLain, that's the silliest thing you ever thought of in all the born days of your life.

He will probably marry Miss Emily Trent. We (the children and I) don't think she's nice enough for him but if he likes her, we'll give him our blessing. I don't think she likes us very much though she has come to see us twice and invited Gay to her house for luncheon one day. Gay is lovely to her because she wants to be a bridesmaid. As though she could! Why, you know, Bruce, Gay couldn't even spell it.

So you see you've been very silly, Bruce.
But I love you in spite of that. I love you
so much that sometimes it's like an ache
and sometimes it's like music and sometimes I just want to cry. You do believe
me, don't you? If you don't I'll probably
drown myself in the fountain in the conservatory. No, I couldn't. There isn't
enough water and, besides, the goldfish
might be offended. But I would do something desperate. I love you so very
much. . . .

And Bruce wrote to Barbara—

. . . I was silly, darling. Will you
forgive me for writing you such a snooty
letter? If you don't, I'll break into the
fruit store some night and eat all the
bananas and die of indigestion.

The silver flute (you know, darling, it
isn't a flute but just my old guitar) is
learning new songs for you. Here's one
that it played to-night—

> " One small table, dear,
>   And two small chairs.
> A lazy parrot for a pet,
>   The kind that never swears.
> And heart-shaped gates to keep away
>   The world and all its cares
>   From one small table, dear,
>   And two small chairs."

The parrot's name is Minerva because
she looks so very wise. The table came
from a second-hand store and the chairs
are rickety as to legs. But the gates are in
good condition. I love you very much.

CHAPTER VI

I

B RUCE was coming for Christmas.

Barbara asked Stephen if she might invite Bruce, as she sat facing him across a small table in a tearoom on Chestnut Street one afternoon a week before Christmas.

"Who is Bruce?" Stephen asked, when she had shyly made the request and sat waiting for his answer, her hands clasped tightly under the edge of the table.

"He's a friend of ours," she answered, wanting to tell him all about Bruce, wondering why she found it a difficult thing to do. "Father liked him."

"An artist?"

"He will be—sometime." Her voice was warm with enthusiasm. "Father said he has a great deal of talent."

"Young or old?"

"About twenty-five, I guess."

She said twenty-five as though it were not so very

young. Stephen felt an odd sort of pang. There were times when it did not please him to be reminded of his age.

This was one of the times. They had been shopping all day—presents for the children, a fur neckpiece for Martha in Provincetown, gifts for the relatives. He had enjoyed shopping with Barbara. He enjoyed looking at her across the small intimate table. Her cheeks were flushed, her lips were red, her eyes were dark and shining. Her hair was pinned in at the nape of her neck because he liked it that way. The frock of honey-colored wool, the soft fur jacket, the hat with the turned-back brim were smart and very becoming.

She had an air of distinction. There were other pretty girls in the crowded tearoom. But, somehow, they all looked alike. You could tie them together, he thought, and sell them in bunches for fifty cents. Barbara was different, as natural as the color in her cheeks, completely un-self-conscious. He saw admiring glances directed at their table, heard admiring comments. He was very proud of his little fillette.

He had long ago given up any attempt to fit her into one of the pigeonholes in his orderly clear-thinking mind. A child? A woman? He didn't know. He thought of her merely as Barbara. She had come to be very dear to him, gay and amusing, grave sometimes, finding adventure in commonplace things. The gift of laughter. It gave him a jolt, at

times like that, to realize that she was just past
eighteen years old.

"You would like Bruce to come?" he asked,
knowing that he could deny her nothing.

"Oh, yes, Uncle Stephen," she assured him.
"You see his family lives in the west and he
wouldn't have time to go home. Being alone at
Christmas would be dreadful with no one for company except a parrot named Minerva."

"Dreadful!" Stephen agreed.

"The children like Bruce. He just about lived
at our house in Provincetown."

"And you like him, Babbie?"

She looked down at the hand which wore his ring.
Dark lashes curtained her eyes.

"Oh, yes, Uncle Stephen," she said, the pink in
her cheeks deepening to rose.

Why couldn't she tell him all about Bruce? He
understood things so nicely. Sometime she would,
when the visit was over. She couldn't now. There
would have to be explanations. It was nicer to keep
it a secret.

What was she thinking? Stephen wondered,
watching the curve of her lashes against her cheeks.
Was she in love with this boy?

"Invite him for Christmas if you like," he said.
"There's always plenty of room."

The dark lashes lifted.

"You're nice, Uncle Stephen," she said, giving
his hand an affectionate squeeze.

"So are you." Stephen returned the affectionate squeeze. Was she in love with the boy? Again he felt an odd sort of pang. But she was eating a great many sandwiches. Girls, he had been led to believe, lost their appetites when they fancied they were in love.

"Would you like something else, Madame?" the waitress asked, hovering near the table.

Barbara hesitated between fudge cake and coffee éclaires. Her appetite was excellent, Stephen thought, feeling immensely relieved. When the waitress had gone, she smiled at him across the table.

"Did you hear what she called me?" she asked, amused.

"Madame," Stephen teased. "It's that hat. You look grown up to-day."

"Maybe she thinks I'm your wife."

Stephen had thought that, too. It gave him a feeling of pride. He couldn't look like "a nice old man" if the waitress had fancied that Barbara was his wife. There was more than pride in the feeling. There was tenderness, too, and a wistful sort of longing.

"Perhaps," he said and his eyes, under brows that frowned a little, were grave and vaguely troubled. "Perhaps that's what she thought."

Barbara's eyes danced with mischief.

"Isn't that funny?" she said with a gay little wounding laugh.

II

Bruce came on Christmas Eve. Barbara went in town with Thomas to meet him at the station. She was excited when the train came in and happy and frightened, too. What if he didn't look the same? What if she had only imagined the color of his eyes, the way he smiled with his teeth so white in the golden brown tan of his skin? What if she had only imagined Bruce?

He didn't look quite the same. He had lost some of the tan. She had never seen him in an overcoat with a scarf and a hat like other men wore. She saw him before he saw her and he seemed, walking through the crowd around the gate, a nice looking stranger who resembled someone she used to know.

His eyes brightened when he saw her. He smiled and looked a little more like Bruce. If she could touch him, perhaps this feeling of strangeness would vanish. . . .

There were people in the way. Plunging ahead, not watching where she was going, she bumped into a woman who dropped packages and holly wreaths and looked very indignant. The moment they had both anticipated was spent in picking up packages and making apologies to the stout indignant lady.

"Did you have a nice trip?" Barbara asked as they walked through the station. That wasn't what she wanted to say. She hated this feeling of strangeness. She didn't quite know what to do.

"The train was crowded." Bruce hadn't meant to say that. What had they done to her? This pretty young lady so smartly dressed might have been his Babbie's elder sister.

"They are at Christmas, I guess." Barbara felt a lump in her throat. She hadn't thought it would be like this. She had thought that meeting Bruce would be lovely. She kept her hands clasped tightly together inside a small round muff. They wanted to cling to his arm. But he acted so stiff and so very polite.

"Yes," Bruce agreed. "Holidays are bad times to travel." He resented the soft fur jacket she wore, the muff, the smart little frock of honey-colored wool. He resented Thomas, in uniform, the big closed car, the air with which Barbara entered it, as though, already, she was accustomed to luxury. She won't want to live in my studio after this, he thought miserably, loving her, feeling that he had lost her.

It was easier in the car when Thomas had turned his back and they drove out the Parkway in the clear frosty twilight. Bruce kissed her and held her in his arms.

"Are you glad to see me?" he asked.

"Oh, Bruce!"

He thought that she was. He felt her small left hand no longer tucked in the muff.

"It's there," she said, knowing the thought that prompted the gesture. She pulled off a soft suede glove and showed him the ring with the small gold heart.

"That makes me feel better," he said, relaxing against the upholstery. "I'll have to get you another," he added after a moment.

"Why?" she asked, surprised.

"That isn't gorgeous enough for an elegant young lady."

"Bruce!" Her voice reproached him. "I love it," she said, nestling close against him. "I don't want any other. I'll wear it as long as I live."

"Darling!" he said, feeling as though he had found her again.

And—

"Darling," she answered, feeling the strangeness vanish.

She told him about a Christmas box from Martha.

"Candy with hickory nuts," she said, "and the cookies we used to like. And pine tassels, Bruce, and bayberry candles to burn on Christmas Eve. We all cried—even Kit. It smelled exactly like home."

She hadn't changed then, he thought, holding her very close. He told her about a book he was illustrating, "so we won't have to live up over the fruit store," about his work at the art school, about the parrot named Minerva which sang hymns instead of swearing. He gave her the gift he had brought, a bracelet with a golden heart to match the birthday ring.

They were happy together during the short ride out from town. But he felt that he had lost her again when the car turned through the stone gateway and followed the winding drive. The lawns seemed enormous to Bruce. The house with its banked evergreens and long lighted windows was a vast dark shape against the deepening twilight. He had not thought it would be so grand.

"I'm frightened," he said, when the car stopped at the entrance and Thomas sprang down to open the door.

"Silly!" she whispered, holding fast to his hand.

The touch of her hand couldn't banish the feeling that he had lost her again. It persisted through the children's noisy welcome, through a dinner which seemed endless to Bruce in spite of Stephen's efforts to make him feel at home. He appreciated the efforts but he resented Stephen who looked younger than he had hoped and very much more attractive.

"Isn't he lovely?" Barbara asked as they left the dining-room with its silver and mahogany, its flowers and tall pale candles.

"Who?" Bruce asked, though he knew very well whom she meant.

"Uncle Stephen."

Bruce was jealous of the shine in her wide dark eyes. He was jealous of the question.

"It was kind of him to let you invite me," he said stiffly, knowing that he had hurt her, wanting to hurt her because he, himself, was hurt.

He was sorry a moment later but then it was too late. He could not find her again, though she was there beside him, small and very lovely in a frock of golden brown velvet. Bruce hated himself for his jealousy. He could do nothing about it.

It was an unhappy evening for them both. They trimmed a tree for the children in the schoolroom, talking gayly, avoiding each other's eyes. If they might be alone, Bruce thought, wanting to apologize, wanting to find her again.

But they were not alone for a moment. The schoolroom, this evening at least, was the center of the house. Henry staggered in and out with packages. Sarah, stout and scolding, puffed down from the attic with boxes of ornaments which had trimmed trees for Stephen and Natalie. Aunt Edith made excuses to visit the schoolroom. Alfred came up with ropes of laurel and a cluster of mistletoe. There was no opportunity for Bruce and Barbara to be alone.

Stephen watched them and wondered. Bruce was a nice looking boy, he thought, and seemed to be on intimate terms with the Thornes. But Barbara wasn't in love with him. He felt that he would know it if she loved this nice looking boy with the charming manners and somewhat shabby clothes. Stephen, as Aunt Edith observed, had much to learn about women.

When the tree was trimmed, Barbara, Stephen and Bruce sat around the library fire. Martha's bayberry candles burned in the windows under the holly wreaths. Henry brought sandwiches and thimble-sized glasses of wine. Stephen was charming to Barbara's guest. If he would leave them alone, Bruce thought, looking at Barbara curled in an armchair beside the fire, wanting to kiss the dimple that woke with her gay little smile.

If Uncle Stephen would leave them, Barbara thought, wanting terribly to be alone with Bruce. He seemed so distant and far away in the chair across from her on the other side of the hearth. What excuse could she make? But excuses wouldn't be polite to Uncle Stephen. She twisted the ring on her finger but she couldn't hear the tinkling sound through Uncle Stephen's voice.

There was no opportunity to be alone. Natalie and Bob, returning from a party, came in at midnight with presents for the children. They stayed almost an hour. And then it was time to go to bed.

" To-morrow," Bruce thought, saying good-night to Barbara, being polite to Stephen.

" To-morrow," Barbara thought, saying good-night to them both, climbing the stairs to the room where Gay slept with visions of presents filling her untroubled dreams.

But " to-morrow " was just as bad. There was no opportunity to be alone. The children claimed the early part of the day. There was company for dinner; Natalie and Bob, Emily and Professor Trent, Aunt Edith's friend Mrs. Beach with her plump pink chins and ropes of pearls cascading over her bosom.

It was an elaborate dinner and lasted a very long time. When it was over, Barbara and Bruce escaped to the conservatory.

"Are you sure there is no one here?" Bruce asked, pretending to look behind the ferns and under the orange trees.

"No one but the love birds and us." Barbara dimpled and smiled. She loved Bruce when he teased. She loved him so, his deep blue eyes, his friendly smile, his hair that was the color of beech leaves in the fall.

"It doesn't seem possible." Bruce found a seat sprayed over with trailing vines. "I never saw a house so full of furniture and people."

"It is always." She sat beside him, glad that they were alone, wanting to make up for all the interruptions. "Must you go to-day?" she asked, a wistful expression in her eyes.

"The eight o'clock train," he said.

Already it was growing dark. They had so little time. He held her close, trying to find her again, if only for a moment.

"Come with me, Babbie," he said. She was so small and very dear lying against his heart. . . . "A bird nestles in your hand, yours to keep for always. Open your hand and the bird is lost in the sky." . . . "Couldn't you, Babbie dear?"

"To-day?"

" Why not? " Reasons seemed unimportant when he held her in his arms.

" I can't, Bruce." Her eyes were wistful but her chin was very firm. " I can't while the children are here."

" When can you? "

" Soon, I guess." She sighed and lifted her head from his shoulder.

Bruce heard the sigh, felt her drawing away from him.

" Don't you want to? " he asked, frightened and hurt by the soft little quivering sigh. " Have you changed your mind? Don't you want to marry me, Babbie? "

" I haven't. I do," she assured him.

He felt that the words lacked conviction.

" You needn't do it from a sense of duty," he said stiffly, bitterly. " A lady, even a very young lady, has a right to change her mind."

" Bruce! " Her voice reproached him.

" I can't give you things like this." His troubled glance included the orange trees, the fountain splashing into its basin, the smart little frock she wore. " It would be a come-down to live with me over the fruit store up four flights of dingy stairs."

" You know it's not for me," she said very close to tears. " It's because of the children, Bruce."

He didn't know. He couldn't be sure.

" Are you sure? " he asked, wanting to hurt her because he was being so terribly hurt.

She couldn't answer the question because of a lump in her throat. She left the seat and stood looking out through the glass into the frosty twilight. Bruce didn't believe her! She felt small and cold and miserable. The evergreens on the lawn, the thorny hedge, blurred and ran together as the tears came.

Bruce saw her tremble, he heard a choked little sob. Tenderness conquered the bitter thoughts. She was so small, so very dear, too small and dear to be hurt. He went to her swiftly, drew her into his arms.

"Babbie!" he said brokenly. "I'm sorry. Of course I know. I shouldn't have asked you that question."

She clung to him, sobbing. He soothed her with gentle words, brushed the soft hair back from her brow.

"I can't bear it when you don't believe me." She lifted a face damp with tears. "I love you so very much."

"I know." Bruce wiped away the tears. "I didn't really doubt you. But I've wanted you so. And this house. It's just that I've been so afraid of losing you. Will you forgive me, sweet?"

The wide brown eyes forgave him. She smiled an April smile.

"Quarrelling has its advantages," she said, standing on tiptoe to press her cheek against his. "It's so much fun to make up."

III

Emily and Stephen sat before the library fire.
They were alone except for the little professor, pot-
tering among the books at the other end of the room.
Barbara had gone with Bruce to the station. Natalie
and Bob had taken Gay to the theatre. Kit and
Jamie were gloating over their treasures in the fes-
tive schoolroom upstairs. Aunt Edith and her friend
Mrs. Beach were playing double Canfield in the music room beyond the library and dipping, at intervals,
into a box of assorted bonbons. Quiet, after a
strenuous day, filled the comfortable fire-lit room.

Emily had looked forward all day to this interval
with Stephen. She had tried not to be disappointed
because his gift to her had been books. They were
lovely, of course, slim volumes of poetry bound in
limp gray leather with lettering done in silver.
Stephen had charming taste. But she would have
liked something more personal. She kept hearing
Barbara's voice . . . " Uncle Stephen! Don't
you know that you shouldn't have given me seventeen
Christmas presents! . . ."

The interval alone with Stephen was not proving
to be all that she had hoped for. She found it increasingly difficult to find subjects for conversation
that were of mutual interest. She had never experienced that difficulty before —— Well, yes,—before the children came. Their tastes had been simi-
lar. Conversation with Stephen had been easy and

delightful. There had been, in those pleasant days, no long difficult pauses. "I had no idea it was so late," Stephen used to say at the end of an evening with her.

Now nothing seemed to interest him except the children. Emily was heartily sick of the Thornes. But because that was the only way to hold his attention, she spoke of them kindly with a show of humorous affection.

"Is this young Mr. MacLain a *special* friend of Barbara's?" she asked, hoping that such was the case.

The question coincided with the question in Stephen's mind.

"They are all fond of him," he said, resenting the curiosity in Emily's low voice. "He has spent his summers in Provincetown. He was their father's friend."

"It wouldn't be surprising if he *was* interested in Barbara," Emily said, wanting to please Stephen and hold his attention. "She is a very pretty girl."

She saw that she hadn't pleased him. He frowned, his brows drawn down over his pleasant gray eyes.

"Barbara is a child," he said with a note of impatience in his voice. "She's just past eighteen."

"But Stephen," Emily said, nettled by the impatient tone, "a girl may be a woman at eighteen. She's old enough to be in love with the boy."

Stephen moved restlessly in the armchair beside the hearth. Emily, he thought, was right about it, perhaps. Why should he mind? The boy was a nice enough chap. He was sure that the relatives would not permit her to marry him unless he could take care of her properly. Why should he refuse to admit that Babbie loved this boy?

But he did refuse to admit it. He stared into the fire, his eyes grave and troubled. She had come to be so dear to him. He loved her as though she were his child. Did he? He didn't know.

"Stephen," Emily said, after an interval of silence, "I should like to ask your advice about a decision I must make."

"Yes?" He gave her his partial attention. It was impossible to give her all of it. His mind was filled with a maze of confusing thoughts. "Yes?" he repeated, looking at her through the flickering firelight.

"Aunt Ada Fairchild, my mother's sister, has asked Father and me to make our home with her," Emily said, carefully choosing her words. "She lives in Winchester, Virginia. Do you think it would be a sensible plan?"

"Excellent," Stephen said, before he had considered what might lie behind the question.

Emily looked down at her hands folded quietly in her lap. Stinging tears filled her eyes. She had hoped that he would protest against her going away. She had hoped that the suggestion would make him realize that he wanted to keep her here. It wasn't working that way.

"Would you be happy there?" Stephen asked, feeling that his immediate reaction to the suggestion had not been what she had hoped. His conscience troubled him vaguely. What had Emily expected? How far had he gone that evening in the conservatory before the children came? He had never been quite sure.

She forced back the tears to save her pride.

"'Shady Lawn' is a lovely old place," she said trying to sound enthusiastic.

It had been once, she thought, though now it was down at the heels. Aunt Ada was a querulous old lady crippled with rheumatism. She knew that it was not a desire for their company that had prompted Aunt Ada to invite them. She wanted someone to take care of her. But it was hard to make ends meet on the income her mother had left. And if Stephen did not ask her to marry him, nothing made very much difference.

To save her pride, she painted, for Stephen, a lovely picture of "Shady Lawn." He should know that she had ancestors, too.

Her gallantry was entirely wasted on Stephen. He believed in the picture of "Shady Lawn." He thought it would be an excellent idea. His conscience ceased to trouble him. Emily seemed to be delighted with the arrangement. Too delighted. He felt a little hurt as well as greatly relieved.

"I'll miss you," he said so gently that the tears spilled over her cheeks.

The tears distressed him. He felt guilty and embarrassed.

"I'm not sure." She controlled her voice with an effort. "It means losing our independence. Father and I have had a happy home."

He doubted that. He appreciated her loyalty. He knew, all at once, what she had expected him to say. Pity for her lay like a weight on his heart.

"Don't decide at once," he said, watching her fingers twist a long string of crystal beads. "Take a little time. I'm not sure that we can spare you."

The gratitude in her eyes increased his feeling of guilt. Why didn't he ask her to marry him? He had wanted to once. What if the children had, for a time, given him new interests, disturbed the orderly pattern of his life? The children, soon, would be gone. He didn't suppose that he had changed fundamentally. Emily loved him. That was obvious. People expected it. Why didn't he do the decent thing?

There was a moment when he might have asked her the question she ached to hear. But the moment passed. Barbara, her cheeks nipped pink by the frosty air, her eyes shining like stars, came into the room.

"Bruce told me to thank you again," she said, "for being so nice to him."

"That's all right," Stephen said, happy at the

thought of her pleasure. He did not look at Emily.
He looked at Barbara's vivid face framed in tendrils
of soft brown hair.

" I thank you, too," she said. " You're nice, Uncle Stephen."

There was a rattling sound. Emily's chain had
snapped. The crystal beads, like small bright tears,
scampered across the floor.

CHAPTER VII

CHRISTMAS was over and Kit was well. Stephen no longer had an excuse for keeping Barbara and the children. But he was reluctant to send them away. He did not like to think of missing that hour before dinner in the schoolroom. He did not like to think of coming home in the evening without Barbara there to meet him and Jamie plunging downstairs with " Chips " at his heels and Kit coming out of the library with a book in his hand and Gay lifting her pretty face for his evening kiss. All of life seemed savorless when he thought of sending the children away.

But he realized, as the January days passed, that he must do something about them. The children should be in school. He looked up schools for Gay and Jamie. Somewhat to his own surprise, he interviewed headmasters and marcelled ladies with gracious manners. Kit should have a tutor at home and go in to art school twice a week. He had not made up his mind to keep them. But it gave him a certain satisfaction to be thinking of schools and tutors and music lessons. He wondered if, after all, he had been meant for a family man.

Did he want to become responsible for them? That was a question he asked himself many times without finding a satisfactory answer. He was sure that they wanted to stay. Their eyes, since Christmas, had followed him wistfully. The relatives would make objections. He thought he could manage them. Aunt Edith, too, would object. He was not quite sure that he could manage Aunt Edith.

Did he want to accept the responsibility? There were times when it seemed absurd, when he went home in the evening determined to pack them off the next day. He never succeeded. Seeing them, hearing their voices, feeling the warmth of their affection, he knew that he could not do it then. "To-morrow," he would think. "To-morrow" never came.

Miss Finch, at the office, had reasons for wondering what had happened to Mr. Drake. He couldn't seem to keep his mind on business at all. He forgot appointments and left the office at odd hours without a word of explanation. She often found him poring over school catalogues with pictures in them of swimming pools and hockey fields and boys or girls on horseback. "You never know," she hinted darkly to her sister. "All men have their secrets, I guess." Miss Finch, what with this and that, was finding the office quite exciting.

Aunt Edith expected Stephen to do something about the children. She did not speak of it because, as she told her friend Mrs. Beach, it was Stephen's house and she had made it a rule not to meddle in his affairs. But Stephen felt her disapproval. She had Bessie serve her dinner in her room. She developed headaches due, so Stephen was led to infer, to having three children in the house. She talked of a Mediterranean cruise or a visit to California.

The children wondered and waited. Would Uncle Stephen let them stay? They invented a game which they called " Straws to Show Which Way the Wind Blows," from one of Martha's sayings.

" He had a school catalogue in his overcoat pocket," Gay would report at a secret conference in the schoolroom. " It was a girls' school. I guess that means me."

Or Kit would tell them, his eyes bright with excitement, " He asked me if I'd like to go to art school. Wouldn't I! Gee! "

" Uncle Stephen thinks boys' camps are a good idea," Jamie reported one evening. " We talked about them this afternoon. Do you suppose dogs are allowed? "

Barbara said Uncle Stephen had asked her if Gay ought to join a dancing class or was it more important to concentrate on the spelling?

" Dancing class! " Gay squealed, bouncing up and down on the sagging springs of the sofa.

"Spelling!" Kit decreed, looking sternly at Gay.

"A little of both, I think," Barbara said with an air amusingly maternal. "If Uncle Stephen will let us stay."

There were straws to show an unfavorable wind as well.

"Uncle Stephen says I can take his 'Moby Dick' when I go," Kit was obliged to report.

"He told his Aunt Edith he wants us to be happy while we're here," Gay said on another occasion.

"He said he'd send me a toboggan," Jamie reported, "when I told him how much snow there is in Maine."

"But he hasn't really decided," Barbara comforted them. "I can tell by the way he frowns when he looks at us sometimes."

So they swung between hope and despair, never entirely sure which way the wind was going to blow. If Uncle Stephen would keep them, was the beginning or the end of every waking thought.

"Sometimes I think he will," Barbara wrote to Bruce. "Wouldn't that be lovely? But sometimes I don't know. It's a very distracting feeling, like being in a lion's cage and not knowing whether the lion will chew your head off or not. But I think he will more than I think he won't. Only I wish he would decide. I'd feel the same way about the lion. . . ."

And then it was decided. Stephen came home one evening looking tired and pleased and a little uneasy as well. He had been away over night—on a business trip, he said. He had presents for the children and some very important news.

"I saw Aunt Josephine," he said, when the boisterous welcome had subsided and the presents had been admired.

"Our Aunt Josephine?" The color paled from Barbara's face. Her eyes were wide and startled.

"Is she a crotchety old lady?" Stephen asked, pretending to be puzzled.

Barbara nodded.

"Does she wear diamond ear drops and black silk dresses and white net collars with points that stick up under her ears?"

Barbara nodded again.

"Does she live in a house with urns and elm trees on the lawn and carpets with roses inside?"

Again Barbara nodded.

"Then I guess it was your Aunt Josephine," Stephen said with a smile.

"What did she say?" the children chorused and then were very still.

"She said you've been badly brought up." Stephen looked at Barbara, at Kit and Gay and Jamie. "She said you had no idea of gratitude. She said I was either very brave or utterly a fool."

"But why, Uncle Stephen?" Barbara's hands clasped each other tightly.

"Because," Stephen told them, "I asked her if I might keep you."

They couldn't believe it at first. He was obliged to tell them again.

" You mean we're to live with you? " Gay asked, ready to bounce on the sofa springs.

" Yes," he answered, rumpling her bright brown curls.

" All of us? " That was Kit, a flush in his thin dark cheeks, his hazel eyes very bright.

" All of you."

" ' Chips,' too? " Jamie asked, preparing to let out a whoop.

" What would we do without ' Chips '? "

The whoop was worthy of a feathered brave on the warpath. It broke the breathless suspense. The children fell upon Stephen with joyous shouts. " Chips " barked in a frenzy of excitement and wagged his stumpy tail. The springs of the old red sofa creaked in a threatening way. The windows rattled. The coals seemed to dance in the grate.

" Aunt Josephine was right," Stephen said when he had emerged, somewhat rumpled, from the lusty strangling embraces. " You're a tribe of little savages. You have no proper respect for your elders."

" Do you want us to be respectful? " Barbara asked, watching the performance with a happy shine in her eyes.

" I like little savages."

Stephen had surrendered himself to the charms of the four Thornes.

CHAPTER VIII

I

A UNT EDITH did not button her lips when Stephen told her he had decided to keep the children. She had a great deal to say, sitting in her room that evening after the children had gone to bed, a card table open across her knees, the chocolate which she always drank before retiring growing cool in its porcelain pot painted with fat pink rosebuds.

Stephen was accepting a grave responsibility, Aunt Edith said, neglecting her bedtime game of solitaire for a matter, less soothing, certainly, but of far greater importance. Rearing children was not an obligation to be so lightly assumed. It was neither wise nor necessary. The children's relatives were able and willing to care for them. Stephen, in her opinion, had taken leave of his senses. Had he considered the possible complications?

"Complications?" Stephen asked, wandering restlessly among Aunt Edith's chairs and footstools and tables and knick-knacks. "I want the children. They want to stay. It all seems fairly simple."

"Of course they want to stay." Aunt Edith shuffled the cards with a rippling sound that was like a sigh. "Has it occurred to you," she asked, "that Barbara might have known in advance that you could give them every luxury and advantage?"

Stephen halted midway between the canopied bed and a chaise-longue upholstered in mauve brocade.

"You mean," he asked, "has it occurred to me that she might have looked up my financial rating?"

"Exactly."

Stephen laughed.

"She doesn't know there are such things," he said.

"I'm not so sure." The laugh did not improve the state of Aunt Edith's mind.

"I am," Stephen said curtly.

"It's possible that she might have." He needn't be so touchy, she thought. She was thinking only of him. It would be disturbing for her, of course, to have the children here. But it would be worse for Stephen. Why hadn't he married Emily? She would have been willing to endure the little professor. That would have been a dignified arrangement, at least. Poor Stephen! Why couldn't the children have stayed in Provincetown where they belonged?

"Not Babbie," Stephen said. "She's an impulsive child. She came to me because there was no one else. She thought only of keeping the children together."

"She isn't a child." The expression in Stephen's

eyes alarmed Aunt Edith. "I was married," she said with great dignity, "when I was just past eighteen."

"She's a very dear little girl."

"Really, Stephen——" Again Aunt Edith shuffled the cards with a sound that was like a sigh.

"She sees people so clearly," Stephen said, thinking of Barbara, wanting to defend her. "She knows it is best for the children to let them grow up together. She's right about it, too." Stephen kicked a footstool out of his way and continued to pace across the soft rose-patterned rugs.

"Spare the furniture, please."

Stephen ignored the rebuke.

"I can't hand them over to those relatives," he continued earnestly. "Babbie trusts me. I can't let her down. She's so small and plucky and helpless."

His voice was gentle. Aunt Edith looked up.

"You're in love with her, Stephen," she said. She had not meant to put the thought into words. But Stephen exasperated her beyond endurance, being so foolish about the girl. He had a mooning look in his eyes whenever he mentioned her name. Stephen! It was more than Aunt Edith could stand.

"That's absurd!" Stephen frowned, his brows drawn down over his angry eyes.

"It has happened before." Aunt Edith's fingers continued to shuffle the cards. It was true, she thought. Stephen had not escaped. Forty, she had heard, was a very dangerous age.

"Do you think that?" he asked, looking at her from under darkly scowling brows.

"I do, indeed." No use contradicting herself, Aunt Edith thought. She was glad she had put the thought into words. Perhaps Stephen could be made to realize that he was making himself ridiculous.

"Why?"

"There must be some reason why you should want to keep these children, a reason other than kindness and a desire to make them happy."

"You haven't a high opinion of me, have you, Aunt Edith?" Stephen asked quietly.

"That seems a strange sort of question." Aunt Edith rippled the cards. "It isn't unnatural, I suppose, to fall in love with a pretty girl."

"You make me feel as though I had taken advantage of the confidence of a child."

"A child? Well, really, Stephen ——"

"Do you think that, Aunt Edith?"

"I have known you for some time, my dear," Aunt Edith said. "I can't think that you would completely disorganize your life unless there was a reason."

There was a reason, of course. He might have told Aunt Edith that he had loved Barbara's mother. But he did not want to tell her. He was tired of explanations. He said "Good-night" and walked out of the room.

Aunt Edith sat in the puffy armchair, thinking, rippling the cards with a sound like a lingering sigh.

Then she pushed back the card table and walked across the room to her desk. When she returned to the chair, she spread out on the table a variety of tourist catalogues and time-tables and folders. With a small gold pencil she traced a leisurely journey across the continent. She made notations and added rows of figures. At intervals, she unbuttoned her lips to sigh.

II

Stephen told Natalie the story the next afternoon. She sat beside the library fire when he returned from the office, still irritated by the interview with Aunt Edith, feeling decidedly out of sorts. He suspected that Aunt Edith had sent for Natalie and had told her the distressing news. What did Natalie think about it all? Was he in for another unpleasant interview?

He found, to his great relief, that he wasn't. Natalie smiled at him lazily from the low chair beside the hearth, her ankles crossed on an ottoman, the smoke from her cigarette curling in rings above her sleek dark head.

"Where are the children?" Stephen asked.

"Bob took them to the Zoo," she answered. "They ought to be back pretty soon."

"May I have some tea?" Stephen dropped into the chair on the opposite side of the hearth and stretched out his legs to the fire.

"You need something stronger than tea. Sherry," Natalie said to Henry hovering at the door.

"Sherry?" Henry looked doubtful.

"Aunt Edith won't catch us." Natalie smiled at Henry. "She's in her room recovering from a shock. Be a lamb, Henry, and trot it out. You look tired, Stephen," she added, when Henry had disappeared. "Was Aunt Edith very unpleasant?"

"Rather," he said, returning her lazy smile.

"She considers it a calamity." Natalie tapped the ashes from the tip of her cigarette.

"A tragedy, no less."

"There was an old woman who lived in a shoe," Natalie teased affectionately. "Poor, poor Stephen!"

Stephen relaxed in the soft deep chair. He had never known Natalie well. The difference in their ages had not encouraged intimacy. When he was a junior in college, she was still wearing socks. But he found it pleasant to sit with her beside the fire. He needed to talk to someone. Natalie was intelligent. She saw things clearly, he thought.

Henry returned with the wine, and glasses like bubbles on slender stems. Stephen sipped it gratefully. He had not realized how tired he had been all day. Aunt Edith had disturbed him. He hadn't slept very well last night.

Now he felt soothed and rested. Natalie talked amusingly in a low lazy voice. The fire, the wine, the gathering twilight invited confidences.

"Aunt Edith thinks I'm in love with Barbara," Stephen said, breaking a comfortable silence.

Natalie looked at him through the firelight, an amused little smile curving the corners of her lips but she said nothing.

"She thinks," Stephen continued, "that I could have no other possible reason for wanting to keep the children. It makes me feel as though I have taken advantage of a child."

"A child, Stephen? Barbara is eighteen." Natalie remembered that, at eighteen, she hadn't considered herself a child. There had been Jimmy Lee. She had been engaged to Jimmy Lee, without Aunt Edith suspecting it, for almost a month and a half.

"Of course in some ways she isn't," Stephen admitted, his eyes troubled and grave. "She's never had time to be really young. Aunt Edith shouldn't leap to conclusions, though. Babbie thinks I'm a nice old man. I think she's a dear little girl. Anything else is absurd."

"Are you in love with her, Stephen?" Natalie asked quietly.

He told her the story, then. He told her about the Barbara he had loved a very long time ago.

"So you see," he said when he had finished, "if you and Aunt Edith must have one, there *is* a reason why I can't let the children go."

"A very good reason," Natalie said gently. It was strange to think that Stephen, always so quiet and reserved, should have been capable of romance.

"It isn't only that," Stephen added, a little embarrassed at having told the story. "It's the children themselves. They're nice youngsters. They'll keep me from getting too stodgy. I like having a family, although it is distracting at times."

"Poor Stephen!" Natalie crossed swiftly to his chair, rumpled his hair in a lazy caress, lightly kissed his cheek. "I'm for you and the children," she said. "I have just discovered that you are rather a dear."

"A mutual discovery." He smiled and pressed her hand.

They had no opportunity for further talk. The front door opened. There were sounds of footsteps in the hall and shouts for "Uncle Stephen." The children and Barbara burst into the room, laughing, eyes bright, their cheeks nipped pink by the cold. The quiet was broken by gay excited voices—

"The elephant had a baby, Uncle Stephen! Its name is Annabelle."

"Aren't the monkeys lovely? They look like weazened old men."

"Will a snake's back break, Uncle Stephen, if you make it walk in a straight line? Kit says ——"

"What makes bears smell so dreadfully? Don't they ever take baths?"

"Aren't zebras silly looking? Like mules all painted with stripes!"

Stephen was lovely with the children, Natalie thought, watching them surround him like a swarm

of chirping locusts. Did she imagine that his eyes
turned most frequently to Barbara, sitting demurely
amused in the big chair? Stephen was right. She
was a child. Her eyes, under the turned back brim
of the smart little hat, were younger than Jamie's.
A lovely child. Stephen was more than twice her
age. She felt, all at once, close to Stephen, afraid
for him. There was something in his eyes. She
didn't want him to be hurt.

"Aunt Edith started something," she said to Bob
as they drove home after dinner.

"What?"

"You remember the old lady who told the children not to put beans up their noses?"

"What connection has that ——?"

"Aunt Edith told Stephen that he is in love with
Barbara."

"Is he?"

"I'm not quite sure." Her voice was troubled.
"Yes," she added, "I think he is."

"Don't blame him. So am I."

"Bob!"

"Jealous?" he teased. "She is a sweet kid, Nat."

"But Stephen is twice her age."

"Worried about it?"

"A little worried, Bob."

"What has become of the Pussy Cat and the
Owl?"

"They've gone to sea," Natalie laughed. "In a
beautiful pea-green boat."

" Really? "

" Aunt Edith thinks so. She says Stephen failed
to do his obvious duty."

" Swell! Too much obvious duty has wrecked
many a good man's life. . . . They're nice kids,
Nat."

" Yes," she agreed. " I hope Stephen isn't in love
with Barbara, though."

" Still worried? "

But she wasn't worried, though she felt guilty
about it. Bob was driving with his left hand. His
right arm held her closely. Her cheek was against
his sleeve.

III

The postman, one morning, brought a note to
Stephen from Emily—

> DEAR STEPHEN,
>   I have decided to take your advice.
> We are packing up and will leave for
> Virginia very soon. Will you come to see
> us before we go? Father will be incon-
> solable if he does not have an opportunity
> to bid you good-bye.
>   How are the children? I have heard
> that you are to keep them. They are lucky
> kiddies.
>
>   Always your friend,
>   EMILY.

Stephen meant to call at the apartment on the outer fringe of Rittenhouse Square. But there were many things to claim his attention besides the work at the office; day-schools for Gay and Jamie, a tutor for Kit, the left upper wing of the house to be done over for the girls who certainly couldn't use, permanently, that vast draughty room with the canopied bed. He interviewed decorators. He carried in his pockets samples of chintz and wall-paper which fell out at unexpected moments. He shopped with Gay and Barbara. It was amusing. It consumed a great deal of time.

And then there were the relatives. He dictated to Miss Finch soothing letters to Uncle Herbert and Aunt Lola and Cousin Julia in Maine. He was obliged to make a second trip to Providence to assure Aunt Josephine that he was a trustworthy guardian for the children. He felt that, on the whole, they were relieved. The questions, the investigations were merely to satisfy their own self-importance.

Aunt Lola wrote plaintive letters to Gay. But Gay liked being at Uncle Stephen's. Aunt Lola's letters made no impression. Stephen suspected that the plump little lady comforted herself by telling the story to her friends on the veranda of the Florida hotel.

Then, too, there was Aunt Edith. She let him feel daily the weight of her disapproval. If it hadn't been for Barbara, Stephen thought, she would have accepted the situation. She was fond of the children, especially fond of Gay. But she resented Barbara. She told him that she planned to visit her friend Fanny Poole in California as soon as arrangements could be made.

Stephen felt guilty about Aunt Edith. He brought her gifts. He tried to interest her in his plans for the children. He played double solitaire with her in the evening and took her to concerts and gave her checks for her charities. Aunt Edith did not relent. She had Henry bring down her trunks. She wrote letters to Fanny Poole. She unbuttoned her lips to sigh.

So the busy days passed and Stephen did not visit the apartment on the outer fringe of Rittenhouse Square. Then, one day, a branch of white lilacs in a florist's window reminded him of Emily. It touched him a little to see it there among the red roses wired into heart shapes for Valentine's Day. He watched the clerk pack it into a box with layers of paper. He walked out of the shop and hailed a cab.

But the apartment was vacant. Emily's thin yellow curtains had disappeared. A neat "To Let" card was tucked in the frame of one of the dusty windows. The shades were drawn as though someone had died.

That evening when Miss Finch reached her sister's home she carried under her arm a slim white florist's box.

"Flowers?" her sister asked, frying chops in a small cluttered kitchen.

"Lilacs!" Miss Finch, bursting with pride, arranged them in a glass vase from Woolworth's. "Mmmm! Don't they smell sweet?"

"Somebody must think a lot of you. Lilacs out of season!"

"Mr. Drake gave them to me." Miss Finch's eyes, behind the glasses that pinched on her nose, beamed with shy excited pleasure.

"Well!" said her sister through the sizzling sound of the chops.

"You could have knocked me down with a feather. 'Here's a present,' he said, sort of late in the afternoon. Can you imagine it! Nothing can ever surprise me again. Nothing in the world."

"Well!" said her sister, noting Miss Finch's sprightly manner, the color in her cheeks. "Well!" she repeated and turned the veal chops over.

CHAPTER IX

I

Thornhedge,
February 15th.

DARLING BRUCE,
Isn't it strange that this place should be called "Thornhedge"? Uncle Stephen says the ancestor who named it must have been a prophet because now there are "thorns" inside as well as out. But not very prickly thorns. The children are angelic. It's too good to last. Something will probably happen. I feel as though I am sitting on the edge of a volcano which may blow up any minute. It isn't natural for children to be so good.

It's so odd to think we are going to stay. I can't make it seem real at all. But we are. Isn't Uncle Stephen lovely? Gay and Jamie are going to school. Gay goes to Miss Carey's and Jamie to a boys' school, sort of in the country not far from here. Thomas takes them every morning and goes for them in the afternoon. I feel sorry for Miss Carey because of Gay's spelling. She will probably be dreadfully shocked. And Jamie's arithmetic isn't what it ought to be. There were a great many

" bumps of knowledge " left out of us when we were made. All of us except Kit. He's as bumpy as a squash with all the things he knows.

Kit has a tutor named William Jones who comes every morning for lessons. Mr. Jones is taking graduate work at the University and is very intelligent, I suppose, but he has the funniest way of blushing whenever he meets me in the halls. His face gets the color of a tomato and his eyes sort of pop. And he stammers dreadfully saying " Good-morning," or " It's a nice day, isn't it? " Kit says he doesn't during lessons. Isn't that weird?

Kit is going to art school in the city and he's so happy that it makes me want to cry. I hope Mother knows about us. And Father, too. We can't be grateful enough to Uncle Stephen if we all live for a hundred years and try as hard as we can.

It's strange about being grateful. I never could be to Aunt Josephine or the relations—because they expected it, I guess. Uncle Stephen doesn't. He just wants us to be happy and so I feel grateful all the time. So do the children. It's a lovely sort of feeling.

Uncle Stephen is having some rooms done over for Gay and me. There are two of them with a bath in between, all green tiles and porcelain and plants that grow under the sea painted on the walls. I shall feel like a mermaid whenever I take a bath. Will you love me just the same if my feet turn into a tail?

Gay's room is to have apple-green enamelled furniture and mine is to be ivory. I'd rather have my carved bed that Father made but it wouldn't be polite to suggest that to Uncle Stephen. He might think I didn't approve of his taste. I do. The loveliest chintz for the curtains and chairs and dressing tables with petticoats, and a toilet set for each of us with our initials on them set in squares of silver. Like the old lady in the Mother Goose rhyme I pinch myself, sometimes, to find out if it is really I.

I loved your Valentine. Where did you ever find such a quaint one with lace paper and rosebuds and that cunning silver arrow? But I must make a confession. I slept with it under my pillow last night and now it's all crumpled. Will you forgive me? It was because I wanted so much to see you.

Your Babbie,
who loves you very much.

II

Thornhedge,
February 20th.

BRUCE, DARLING,

No, I haven't told Uncle Stephen about us, yet. It wouldn't be considerate. He's had so many things to bother him. His Aunt Edith has gone to California with three trunks and Bessie her maid and I'm sure it was because of us, though Uncle Stephen pretends it wasn't. But I heard Bessie tell Sarah it

was. She said Aunt Edith said Uncle Stephen had
completely lost his mind and she wouldn't have believed it.

I must say it's a relief to have her gone. She
didn't like me very well. Or any of us, except Gay.
But it's hard for Uncle Stephen because she is his
aunt and she has lived here ever since his father
and mother died. Now *I* sit at the head of the table
and pour Uncle Stephen's coffee and remind the children of their manners and ring the bell for Henry.
I do my hair up now. I simply couldn't sit at the
head of Uncle Stephen's table with it all tumbling
around my shoulders. As it is, I have to slide off
the edge of the chair to reach the bell with my foot.
I'm a cottage-sized hostess, Uncle Stephen says.

And something else has happened to bother Uncle
Stephen. Miss Trent and her father have gone to
Virginia to live. Uncle Stephen isn't going to marry
her, after all, I guess, and that's because of us, too.
If you don't care for children (and I'm sure Miss
Trent doesn't) and they come anyway you " take
them to the Lord in prayer," as Martha says, I suppose, but if you are threatened with four which
aren't your own, you " fold your tents like the Arabs
and silently steal away." That's what Miss Emily
and her father did, though I can't imagine him
dressed like an Arab and riding on a camel. He
looks more like an owl scared out of a tree.

Gay thinks it was noble of Uncle Stephen to sac-
rifice himself for us. She's always talking about

"Blighted beings" and "lovers parted forever."
(She gets such things out of the kind of books Katie
reads. I found "Wife in Name Only" under the
mattress on our bed. Gay can be so silly.) But I
do think it bothered Uncle Stephen. He never acted
very "loverish" to Miss Emily but I guess older
people don't and he's probably "grieving in silence,"
so that we won't feel bad.

So you see, darling, I can't tell him about us just
yet. He depends on me for everything about the
children. It wouldn't be fair to run away and leave
him, especially since it's my fault that we're here
and his Aunt Edith has gone to California and he
has lost his love.

When having a family isn't so new and strange
and his Aunt Edith comes home or he finds somebody else to marry who likes children, I'll tell him.
You do understand, don't you, darling? You do
know that I love you.

BABBIE.

III

Thornhedge,
March 1st.

DEAR BRUCE,

Please don't consider writing to me a duty. I
know that you are busy and can't be expected to
answer three letters in a row. How is the "Portrait of Minerva" progressing? I hope she's a
good model. I wasn't, was I? when you painted me

last summer in Provincetown. I hope Minerva doesn't fidget the way I used to.

The weather is getting to feel like spring. Alfred, our gardener, says that the crocuses will be up pretty soon. There are buds on the maple trees and Jamie has seen three robins.

Gay is to be " Celia," own cousin to " Rosalind " in "As You Like It " which the girls at Miss Carey's are going to present in May. She's so excited about it that she can't sleep at night. Kit is making a pencil sketch of Henry. It's pretty good only he's making the whiskers too fierce. Henry is really a very mild-looking man.

Uncle Stephen took Gay and me to the theatre last night to see " Hamlet." He was a very gloomy person, wasn't he? No wonder Ophelia went crazy. He's going to take us to see " As You Like It " Saturday afternoon so Gay can get some pointers. She probably won't eat a bite from now until Saturday. Gay has a temperamental nature. She may turn out to be an actress instead of marrying somebody rich.

I hope you are well. Don't work too hard.

Your friend,

BARBARA THORNE.

IV

Atlantic City,
March 3rd.

DARLING BRUCE,

Can you ever forgive me for writing such a snippy letter? But I hadn't heard from you for more than a week and I was worried and hurt and dreadfully unhappy. You imagine all sorts of things when you wait for letters which never come and, besides, I haven't a nice disposition. Why didn't you fall in love with one of these Superior Persons who are always sweet-tempered and wise and good? I'm glad you didn't. They must be dull, don't you think so, darling?—Superior Persons, I mean.

You should have had measles long ago. They aren't one of the pleasures to be reserved for old age. And to think of them putting you in the children's ward at the hospital! I loved the sketches—especially the one of your nurse. But I don't believe she's really that homely. I think you made her up just so I wouldn't be jealous. She's probably small and blonde with big baby-blue eyes. You see what a suspicious nature I have. Do you love me just the same?

I felt so mean when your letter came. I wanted to fly to New York and sit by your bed and feed you things with a spoon. But we were just leaving for Atlantic City and so I couldn't very well. Uncle Stephen had to come on business and he brought Gay

and me because Gay was so disappointed about missing " As You Like It " and Uncle Stephen thought
I looked sort of pale. That was because I'd been
worrying about you. But I didn't tell him that. I
said it was " growing pains " because, you know,
Bruce, I am growing up. I can feel it. Perhaps, in
time, I may become a Superior Person. But I hope
you won't ever think I am dull.

Atlantic City is exciting. We're staying at a
gorgeous hotel. You should see Gay enter the dining-room. A princess, no less!! You can imagine
the crown and the ermine train and the pages in moss
green velvet. But the smell of the ocean makes me
homesick. I wish we were back in Provincetown. I
guess a gypsy girl can't ever turn into a Social Butterfly. Uncle Stephen is lovely to me but, somehow,
I'm lonely all the time. I love you very much.

                                        BABBIE.

                        V

                              Thornhedge,
                              March 10th.

BRUCE, DARLING,
        Don't write me letters like that. They make
me so unhappy. I don't love the children more than
I love you. But I can't desert Uncle Stephen now.
It's my fault we are here. I can't just run away
and leave the children on his hands. You see, he
depends on me so. Sometimes, when it isn't all so

new and strange to him, I'll tell him about us. But it wouldn't be grateful now. Please try to understand.

Hasn't the silver flute learned any new songs? You haven't sent me one for so long. It doesn't really matter. I like the old one best. I hear it every night before I go to sleep . . . " I love you, little gypsy girl with the roses in your hair. . . ."

Oh, I do love you, Bruce! But it's all so confusing. Please try to understand.

Your Babbie.

VI

Thornhedge,
March 12th.

No, Bruce. I can't, I can't.

CHAPTER X

I

SPRING came. The maples budded. The grass grew spongy and green. Jonquils and tulips made patches of color in the garden. The lilac bushes were drifts of purple and mauve. The air was charged with sweet uneasy magic.

And then, before it seemed possible, spring was dancing on toward summer. The wind blew gently through the green foliage of the trees. The Japanese maples flaunted their crimson against the pointed spruce. There were peonies in the garden and the rose-bushes were starred with tight little pink-tipped buds. A family of orioles came to live in the bird-house that looked like a Swiss chalet. Bees hummed in the honeysuckle and in the blue wisteria blossoms.

The children lived out of doors. Alfred levelled and rolled the croquet ground bordered with hedges of box. Targets were set up on the lawn under the copper-beech trees. New willow chairs, for lazy reclining, appeared on the terrace behind the house.

The old place took on an atmosphere of gayety and youth.

Stephen's pleasure in the children increased. He liked to come home from the office in the afternoon to find Gay and her friends from Miss Carey's drifting like butterflies over the terrace and lawns. He enjoyed a game of archery with Kit who beamed with shy pleasure over his own increasing skill. He shared exciting discoveries with Jamie. It was pleasant to sit on the terrace and talk to Barbara curled beside him in a low willow chair, to hear the happenings of the day, to ask her opinion on various matters.

She always had an opinion. Her mind, naive at times, at times amazingly mature, was a delight to Stephen. It amused him to watch her consider a question before answering, the pucker soft as a wrinkle in silk between her curving brows. The gestures of her small gay hand were dear to him, her varying moods, her quick response to beauty. There were times when he felt like her father and times when he was obliged to remind himself very sharply that she was a lovely child.

Stephen felt as though he had cast off a number of dreary years. He had no regrets about keeping the children. Even when Aunt Edith's letters arrived, weighted with resignation, he did not repent. Life moved to a quickened rhythm. It seemed to him that he must have been only half alive before the children came. He had thought that he dreaded

changes. He found them, on the contrary, stimu-
lating and pleasant.

He was immensely proud of the children. Gay,
as " Celia " was enchanting. He had felt foolishly
proud, when at the end of the performance, she ran
toward him, stumbling over her Elizabethan train,
and held up her face for his approving kiss. He
wandered into the art school frequently for the
pleasure of hearing that Kit was making remarkable
progress. He took Jamie to a ball game and was
delighted when a man with a stubbly beard and a
battered straw hat said to him, " Your kid knows
the game pretty well."   He understood, now, why
fathers bored their friends by talking about their
families. He found it difficult, on several occasions,
to keep himself from becoming that kind of bore.

There was but one thing to mar his satisfaction.
He felt, as May tripped past in a succession of
balmy days, that Barbara was unhappy. She was
more quiet than she had been in the winter. She
smiled, instead of laughing, an April smile with a
suggestion of tears behind it. She looked at him so
often with a wistful expression in her eyes. He
found her in odd lonely places, beside the lily pond
at the far end of the garden, curled on the schoolroom sofa, walking alone along the winding drive.

" Aren't you happy, dear ? " he asked as they sat
on the terrace one evening after dinner, watching
the fireflies twinkle and darken, darken and twinkle
through the dusk.

"Happy?" He fancied there was a catch in her voice. Her face in the deepening twilight was small and white and troubled.

"I've wondered." He moved his chair closer to hers. "You're so quiet, Babbie. Is something troubling you?"

"No," she said slowly. Then she smiled, the April smile that was close to tears, and slipped her hand into his. "No, Uncle Stephen," she said.

"I want you to be happy." The touch of her hand was disturbing. "Is there anything I can do?"

"You've done so much." She looked up at him, her eyes wide and dark. "I'll always be grateful. Always, as long as I live."

"I don't want you to be grateful," Stephen said gently. "I want you to be happy."

"I am happy," she said.

But she wasn't happy. There was always a lump in her throat and she didn't sleep very well. She hadn't heard from Bruce for nearly three weeks, except a note to tell her that he couldn't get away for a week-end at "Thornhedge." Bruce didn't believe that she loved him. He thought she preferred to stay with Uncle Stephen.

But she couldn't tell Uncle Stephen. It didn't seem grateful or polite.

"It's this lovely weather," she said, instead. "Don't you think spring is sad, Uncle Stephen? It makes a lump in my throat."

She talked brightly enough after that. She led him down through the shadows to the lily pond to show him Jamie's pet frog, penned in a moated castle made of stones and twigs and bits of spongy moss. They invented stories about the frog. They laughed and were very gay. But when they returned to the house, Stephen saw that there were traces of tears on her cheeks.

During the days that followed, he watched her closely. Sometimes when she rode with him, her cheeks flushed under the jaunty three-cornered hat, her eyes sparkling with pleasure, he thought that he was mistaken. When she played at archery with Kit, a small and dainty Diana, surprisingly sure and strong, he was confident that the troubled moments were merely moods. She was alert, then, bright-eyed, enthusiastic.

"Look, Uncle Stephen! I hit it! Almost exactly in the center!"

But there were other times when he knew that she was worried about something. Sometimes when she came down to breakfast in the morning, she looked as though she had not slept. He found her one afternoon by the lily pond weeping over a letter.

"It's from Martha," she explained. "Martha says that a storm last winter broke one of our willow branches. I love our willow trees." . . . Bruce had given her the ring with the small gold heart under the willows—

"Oh, Bruce! It just exactly fits!"

"It should. It was made for you. The heart is to match your face."

And the sound of the wind in the willows was a song that was happy and sad. . . .

She was homesick, perhaps, Stephen thought. The gray-shingled house she mentioned so often was very dear to her.

"Would you like to go back?" he asked, wanting to make her happy.

"All of us?"

"We can drive up this summer."

She shook her head.

"Thank you, Uncle Stephen." The lashes that curved against her cheeks were stuck into points by tears. "I don't think I want to—just yet."

He took her to a concert one evening. She seemed to enjoy it at first, but suddenly, when the orchestration became a low accompaniment for the clear silver notes of a flute, he heard through the liquid music, a small heart-broken sob.

"Babbie!" he whispered, startled. "Babbie, what is it?"

"Let's go." She was struggling against the sobs that distorted her face. "Please, Uncle Stephen, let's go."

"What was it, Babbie?" he asked, when they had left the hall and were driving home in the car. "What made you so unhappy?"

"It was the flute, Uncle Stephen," she said in a small weary voice. "I—I couldn't bear it."

The sobs decreased in violence. She drew a long quivering breath.

" I'm sorry I made a scene," she said, slipping her hand into his. " Was it dreadful, Uncle Stephen? "

" Don't think about that." He held her in his arms, felt her hair, soft and silky and faintly scented, brushing across his cheek. He thought that she might explain. She didn't. She curled her fingers around his hand and nestled against his shoulder.

" I'm a lady with nerves." She laughed shakily. " I belong in one of Jane Austen's books."

Perplexed and troubled, Stephen confided in Natalie.

" Babbie isn't happy," he said, finding her on the terrace one afternoon, making new sails for Jamie's boat.

" I've noticed that." Natalie came often to see the children. She was especially fond of Jamie whose heart she had won with the gift of a collar for " Chips." She had noticed that Barbara seemed unhappy. " Why? " she asked, deftly stitching the sails.

" I wish I knew."

Natalie glanced up, touched by the troubled tone in his voice. Stephen was gazing down across the lawn to where Barbara sat on the grass leaning against the trunk of a tree. She wore a pale yellow dress, the color of a primrose, and the late afternoon sunlight, slanting through the foliage of the

tree, brightened her soft brown hair. A book lay
open in her lap. But, from the terrace, she did not
appear to be reading. There was something wistful
in her position. There was a wistful expression in
Stephen's eyes.

"I want her to be happy," he said. "What can
I do?"

"She needs to be more with young people," Natalie ventured to suggest.

"Young people?" A shadow slipped across
Stephen's face. He was frowning a little, his brows
drawn down over his eyes.

"Boys and girls her own age." Natalie knew
that she had hurt him. But she thought she was
right. "You're selfish, Stephen," she continued.
"You can't guard her like a watch-dog. After all,
she's eighteen."

"Perhaps I have been selfish," Stephen agreed.
"Well, what do you suggest?"

"Give a party for her. A dancing party outdoors."

"Lord, Nat!" Stephen groaned. "I don't know
any youngsters."

"I do."

"Will you manage it for me?"

"Gladly." Natalie smiled at Stephen's worried
expression. "There was an old woman ——" she
teased.

"I pity her," Stephen said, "if all of her children
were girls!"

II

There was a moon for Barbara's party, a round June moon that netted the lawns with black and silver shadows. The terrace was floored for dancing. There was an orchestra and a refreshment tent. There were girls in flower-tinted frocks and boys in white flannels and one in an Annapolis uniform tricked out with buttons and braid. There were voices and laughter and hummed snatches of popular songs. There was Barbara in a dancing frock all filmy floating white tulle.

It was going very well, Stephen thought, watching the dancing from an unobtrusive position. Barbara seemed to be having a happy time. Her cheeks were as pink as the rosebuds in her tiny nosegay with its frill of white paper lace. Her eyes shone like misty dark stars. Her silver slippers twinkled. She danced as lightly as though she hadn't a care in the world. How lovely she was in that filmy white frock. Was it necessary for the young cub in the uniform to hold her so closely? This was a dancing party and not a football game.

"Will you dance with me?" Stephen asked through the applause that clamored for an encore.

She turned from the uniform. She slipped into his arms all misty with tulle and glowing cheeks and darkly shining eyes.

"I didn't know you could dance," she said, her hand against his shoulder.

"I manage to get around." Stephen guided her smoothly among the circling dancers. "But I don't know this modern technique," he confessed. "In my day dancing was dancing."

"You're not that old, Uncle Stephen," she said with a gay little laugh.

How old did she think he was? He felt ancient compared with these flippant youngsters who tried so desperately hard to act like men of the world. She was so light in his arms, so graceful, so fragrant. Barbara. Babbie. Dear. . . .

"Happy?" he asked.

"It's a lovely party."

"Happy?" he asked again.

She lifted her face and he saw that there was pain beneath the shining in her eyes. Something troubled her, something that a party could not banish. Babbie. His arm tightened about her. Lovely child. . . .

"Pardon me, sir." That was the uniform, snatching her away.

"It's called 'cutting in,'" Barbara explained, smiling over the shoulder of the uniform. "You can do it, too."

Stephen did not take advantage of the privilege. The boy's respectful "Sir" had put him in his place. She belonged with the youngsters to-night, with the cub in the uniform and the youthful men of the world who snatched her from each other and snatched her back again. Stephen walked to the edge of the terrace where Kit sat on a willow settee watching the dancing he could not share.

"Pretty show, isn't it, Kit?" Stephen asked seating himself beside the boy.

"Great," Kit said, pleased to share his retreat with Uncle Stephen. "Babs is the Queen Bee, too," he added proudly.

"Is she having a nice time?" Stephen asked, his eyes following the small dancing figure in misty white.

"I guess so," Kit said in intimate man-to-man fashion. "Girls like a fuss. Would you care for a sandwich?" he asked, diving under the settee. "I have some tucked away."

"No, thank you, old man," Stephen said with a smile. "But you have one if you like."

"Thanks." Kit set his teeth in a sandwich. "I suppose," he added with his mouth very full, "Babs will be getting married soon."

"What makes you think so?" Stephen asked, feeling a strange pain in his heart.

"Well, she's so pretty." Kit swallowed rapidly. "I've always thought that Babs was lovelier looking than Gay."

"So have I," Stephen agreed. "But about this getting married ——"

"Girls do," Kit observed. "William Jones is in love with her."

"He is, is he?" Stephen frowned. Kit's tutor, William Jones! The infernal brass of that!

"He wrote some poetry about her," Kit continued, varying his banquet with salted almonds and small pink cakes. "It fell out of one of his books. I thought you ought to know because we can't let Babs marry anybody like that."

"You don't think she—returns his affection, do you?" Stephen asked. Certainly, he thought, watching the small dancing figure, Babbie couldn't have been making herself miserable over a fellow like William Jones.

"No," Kit said, contentedly munching. "But she might feel sorry for him. Babs hates to hurt people's feelings."

"I'll attend to that," Stephen said with a degree of emphasis that surprised them both.

"What, Uncle Stephen?" Gay, in apricot taffeta, drifted toward them like a butterfly dancing over a lavender bed. "What will you attend to?"

"This is a private conversation," Kit said with as much dignity as a cheek full of almonds would permit.

Gay ignored the rebuke. She settled herself between them and drew a long blissful sigh.

"This is the loveliest party!" she said.

"Are you having a nice time?" Stephen asked, rumpling her bright brown curls.

"Lovely!" she breathed. "And isn't Bab? The girls are all furious at her."

"Why?" Stephen asked, surprised that anyone could be furious at Babbie.

"Well, look how the boys act about her," Gay said with a glance which told Stephen how little he understood women. "That Susie Monroe is the worst of all."

"Which one is Susie Monroe?" Stephen asked, recalling that she must be the granddaughter of the Mrs. Monroe who was a friend of Aunt Edith's.

"The sort of plump one in the green dress." Gay was pleased to be the bearer of interesting news. "She came with the boy from Annapolis and he's been trying to dance every minute with Babs. Isn't it exciting? I wish I was eighteen."

"Cat!" Kit said severely.

"Well, I just told you," Gay said plaintively, "because I thought you'd want to know."

"I suppose you've been snooping around listening to what people say," Kit observed with a scornful glance for his pretty sister. "You'll probably turn out to be a terrible gossip, Gay Thorne."

Gay's lips trembled.

"I couldn't help it," she said, wilting under Kit's glance. "If I have ears, I can't help hearing what people say, can I? Gracious, do I have to stuff cotton in them or wear ear-lappers or something?"

"You don't have to cry," Kit said, relenting. "Have a cake or a sandwich or something. There's plenty under the bench."

Stephen left them, reconciled, contentedly munching together. Kit's high-handed manner of dealing with Gay usually amused him. But now he had

something else on his mind. Barbara had disappeared. He did not see the small graceful figure in
filmy white among the dancers on the terrace.

"You can't guard her like a watch-dog," he reminded himself. "After all, she *is* eighteen."

But Natalie's comment had no effect. He remembered the hurt he had seen in her eyes. He
walked rapidly down the terrace, under the lanterns,
across the lawn netted with black and silver shadows.

III

He found her beside the lily pond at the far end
of the garden. She looked like a small still statue
seated there, the evergreens dark behind her, her
filmy skirt spraying out on the grass.

"Babbie," he called very gently.

She lifted her face, small and white in the moonlight, framed in silky tendrils of soft brown hair.

"Oh, it's you, Uncle Stephen," she said.

"Who did you think it might be?"

"That sailor."

"The boy from Annapolis?"

"I ran away from him."

"Why?" Stephen asked, seating himself beside
her on the grassy rim of the pond.

"I don't like his hands," she said. "They paw."

"I'll spank him." Stephen seethed with indignation. "I'll spank him buttons and all."

"Oh, no, you won't, Uncle Stephen." Her hand

slipped into his. "I was glad of an excuse. I wanted to run away."

"Don't you like your party?"

"It's a lovely party," she said quickly, afraid that his feelings might be hurt. "But boys aren't amusing. Not very young boys like that."

"Do they seem very young to you?"

"Young and silly." She turned from him with a choked little sob.

"Babbie! You're crying, Babbie."

She did not try to deny it. He drew her into his arms, felt her turn, felt her arms around his neck.

"Can you tell me, dear?" he asked. "It hurts me to see you unhappy. Can't you tell me, Babbie, dear?"

She clung to him, wanting to be comforted, to find some relief for the pain she no longer could bear alone. Her arms tightened about his neck. She could tell him, perhaps, to-night. He would understand. He must understand about Bruce. But she couldn't hurt Uncle Stephen. She wanted him to know that she was grateful, that with all her heart she did love him, too.

Stephen felt her trembling in his arms. He was trembling, too. Had all of this unhappiness been about him? She didn't like the boys who were silly and too young. Did she mean —— He couldn't believe it. The thought turned the world upside down.

"Barbara," he said brokenly.

It was strange that he should call her that. She could tell him now. But he must know that she was grateful.

"I do love you, Uncle Stephen," she said.

And then she knew that she couldn't tell him. He kissed her, not as he had kissed her many times, but in a different way. She knew what the kisses meant. She knew about being in love.

Part Three

CHAPTER I

I

BARBARA lay on the beach, her arms folded under her head, her eyes dreaming up into the cloudless blue of the sky. Kit sat beside her, sketching. At a little distance, Gay in a brief green bathing suit was the center of a noisy chattering group. Jamie and the Parrish twins, freckled and brown as gypsies, were building a miniature golf course. " Chips " and the Parrish Airedale were engaged in a friendly tussle, their frisky feet flinging up showers of sand.

Barbara had forgotten Kit and the children. She lay very still, thinking of many things. Summer was over. This was their last day at Bay Head. To-morrow they would return to " Thornhedge." What then? " When the summer is over," Uncle Stephen had said.

She thought, with a faint confused feeling, of what that might mean. " When the summer is over." She knew, now, that she had tried to hold the days, to keep them from passing too rapidly. Each of them was precious, sunny days, gray days wrapped in blankets of fog, stormy days when the wind blew from the northeast and the breakers pounded against the shore. Another day. Something might happen. Weeks ahead. Passing, passing too rapidly, sunny days, cloudy days, days when the storm wind blew. She could not hold them. They were gone. "When the summer is over," Uncle Stephen had said.

She remembered the day he had said it, the day after her party when Uncle Stephen had kissed her beside the lily pond in that new and frightening way. It was late in the afternoon. She had sat in the library alcove, hidden by the hangings, trying to write a letter to Bruce. She had been trying all day to write the letter, a sad difficult letter, a letter to tell him that she must stay with Uncle Stephen. She hadn't slept well the night before. She was tired, so dreadfully tired. The rain against the window had been soothing. She had always liked the drowsy sound of gently falling rain. She had gone to sleep, tired, so dreadfully tired.

Voices had roused her, Uncle Stephen's voice, the plushy fat-sounding voice of Aunt Edith's friend, Mrs. Beach. She had meant to come from behind the curtains. It wasn't polite to listen to a conversation when no one knew you were there.

And then she had discovered that Mrs. Beach was talking about her. She couldn't come out then. She had been too shy and hurt and ashamed, too sorry for Uncle Stephen.

Susie Monroe, she had heard, had seen Uncle
Stephen kiss her beside the lily pond, Susie Monroe,
the plump girl in the green dress who had come to
the party with the Annapolis boy. Susie had told
her grandmother and her grandmother, a friend of
Aunt Edith's, had told Mrs. Beach. Everybody was
talking, Mrs. Beach reported. She felt it her duty
to tell Stephen. She never shirked a duty, she said,
because it was unpleasant. She pretended to be
sorry and indignant. But Barbara, trembling behind
the curtains, knew that she was pleased and excited
and bursting with importance.

Uncle Stephen had been very angry indeed—
angry but very polite. He had said very little. Barbara knew how he looked, his brows drawn down
over his eyes. She knew, by the tone of his voice,
that he was angry and hurt. She had been so sorry
for Uncle Stephen, hearing Mrs. Beach talk. He
had been kind to her and the children, so wonder-
fully gentle and kind. She wanted to help him,
somehow. There was nothing she could do.

Uncle Stephen, at last, had rung for Henry. Mrs.
Beach had rustled out of the room, leaving behind
her a strong scent of heliotrope and an embarrassing
situation.

Barbara had not meant Uncle Stephen to know
that she had overheard the conversation. She
waited until she thought he had left the room.
Then she stepped out from behind the curtains. He
was there, standing beside the hearth, a cigarette in

his hand, his brows drawn down over his angry eyes. He had looked sorry when he saw her, sorry and angry and hurt.

" You heard? " he had asked.

" I'm sorry, Uncle Stephen."

" Damn them," he had said, meaning Mrs. Beach and Susie Monroe and Susie's gossiping grandmother.

" It was because of the Annapolis boy, I guess," Barbara had said. " Susie didn't like it because he danced with me."

" I'm so terribly sorry." He had looked so sorry and angry that she had wanted to help him.

" People will talk, Uncle Stephen. There's nothing you can do."

" There's one thing," he had said.

She knew what he meant. She could tell by the expression in his eyes. A weight had settled into her heart. If he hadn't kissed her the evening before in that frightening sort of way she would have thought that he meant only to protect her. But he had kissed her. She knew about being in love.

" Barbara ——" he had said.

She had wanted to stop him. Thinking of Bruce, she had wanted to run away. He must have seen that she was confused. He had not touched her. With hand that trembled a little he had lit his cigarette.

" We won't talk about it now," he had said. " When the summer is over ——"

He had taken them to Bay Head with Sarah and a brown cook named Eliza. He had come down only for week-ends. Barbara was grateful for that. Since the evening beside the lily pond, since Mrs. Beach had swept out of the library, it had embarrassed her to be with Uncle Stephen. It hurt her to feel that way. But she couldn't help it no matter how hard she tried.

Uncle Stephen had been as kind as ever. He had not referred to the incident beside the lily pond or to Mrs. Beach who did not shirk an unpleasant duty. He had encouraged her to make friends with the young people at the shore. But his manner had changed. He treated her like a grown-up young lady. He never kissed her as he did Gay or tousled her hair or ducked her under the waves. He never called her Babbie. He called her Barbara now, all the time.

She might have thought that she had imagined that evening beside the lily pond except that, sometimes, he looked at her in a wistful sort of way. One evening she had found him on the veranda smoothing the folds of her evening coat tossed over the back of a chair. There had been something in his eyes. She had slipped away with a lump in her throat. She couldn't hurt Uncle Stephen. He had been so kind to them all.

And now it was September. " When the summer is over," Uncle Stephen had said. . . .

" How's that ? " Kit handed her the drawing and

waited for her comment. It was a sketch of Barbara in her bathing suit, lying there on the sand, her arms crossed under her head. There was something familiar about it.

"Splendid," she said. And then, with a little catch in her voice, "It looks like the things Bruce used to do.'"

"Does it?" Kit asked eagerly. "I hoped it did. Bruce taught me, you know."

Barbara knew. She saw the gray-shingled house in Provincetown, saw Bruce and Kit sketching her as she sat in a deck chair under the willows. Bruce . . .

"Do you know where Bruce is, Babs?" Kit asked, after a moment of silence.

"No," she said, turning her head to avoid Kit's eyes. She didn't know. He had not answered the difficult letter she wrote him, the letter which told him that she must stay with Uncle Stephen. Her following letters had been returned unopened. She had tried to reach him by telephone one night, creeping downstairs to the library after the house was quiet and everyone was in bed.

The voice which answered was unfamiliar. Mr. MacLain had sublet the studio, the voice had said. The voice did not know where he had gone. He had left no forwarding address. Later, she had written to him at Provincetown. The letters were returned to her unopened. Bruce had disappeared without telling her that he understood, without a

consoling word, Bruce who had loved her so
much. . . .

"I should think he would write to us," Kit grum-
bled. "I thought he liked us a lot."

Liked them! . . . "Once there was a gypsy
boy who loved very dearly a little gypsy girl. . . ."

"Remember how he used to take us swimming?"

Barbara nodded, unable to speak because of a
lump in her throat. . . . "He was afraid to tell
her how deeply he loved her because she was a little
girl no higher than his heart and he wasn't sure that
she knew about being in love. . . ."

"And how nice he was when Father died?" Kit
asked, remembering Bruce.

Again Barbara nodded, her lashes wet with tears
which Kit could not see. . . . "The flute knew
only one song. 'I love you, pretty gypsy girl with
the roses in your hair. . . .'"

"Babs," Kit said, after an interval of silence.

"Yes?"

"This is sort of a funny question I'm going to
ask."

"What is it, Kit?"

"Well, I was thinking ——" Kit flushed and
looked embarrassed. "I mean wouldn't it be funny
if you should marry Uncle Stephen?"

"What put that idea in your head?"

"Sarah told Eliza you are." Kit's flush deepened. "Of course I don't listen to servants' talk.
But Gay told Sally Parrish."

"You know how Gay is, Kit."

"Yes, I know." Kit rolled over on his side. "But I was just thinking—wouldn't it be sort of funny, Babs?"

"Would you like it?" Barbara asked.

"I think it would be swell," Kit answered promptly. "Then we could all stay together. You have to marry somebody, I suppose."

"Maybe not."

"Gee, Babs!" Kit's voice held a note of distress. "You don't want to be an old maid!"

"I won't be," she said, smiling faintly. "Not for a year or two." If she wouldn't keep thinking of Bruce. If there wasn't always an aching lump in her throat. . . .

They were quiet after that. Kit modelled figures in the sand. Barbara lay with her arms crossed under her head, her eyes dreaming up into the shining blue of the sky. Where was Bruce? The silver flute didn't play any more. She couldn't hear the high sweet notes no matter how still and breathless she kept, no matter how hard she tried. Bruce had gone. Nothing mattered. Nothing mattered at all. . . .

Kit's voice broke the lazy silence.

"Here comes Uncle Stephen," he said, springing up from the sand. "He's early to-day. I guess that's because we're going home."

Going home! But home was the gray-shingled house in Provincetown. She could never think of

"Thornhedge" as home. They were going back to-morrow. "When the summer is over," Uncle Stephen had said. . . .

II

Barbara saw Uncle Stephen walking toward them down the beach, tall and erect in his bathing suit, tanned by week-ends with them at the shore. She saw Gay leave the chattering group and run to meet him. She saw Jamie racing toward him with "Chips" barking a welcome at his heels. She saw Kit, his face shining with shy excited pleasure, crowding Gay and Jamie aside. The children loved Uncle Stephen. She loved him, too. But she wanted to run away.

"How's my girl?" Stephen asked, dropping down on the sand beside her.

"Fine," she answered, crawling inside the secret shell of herself. She didn't like to hide from Uncle Stephen. But she had to, somehow. It was something she couldn't help.

The children clustered about him. There were many things to discuss. Kit's boat had a broken rudder but there was no use having it mended since they were leaving to-morrow. Sally Parrish had invited Gay to visit her in New York. Did Uncle Stephen think she might go the week-end after next? Jamie had cut his foot on a piece of broken glass. But it wasn't anything much though Sarah predicted lock-jaw. How were Henry and Katie? Had the kittens grown into cats? Did Jamie's pet frog still live in his moated-castle beside the lily pond?

Barbara heard Uncle Stephen's answers, saw and loved his patience with the children. It was lovely to see them together, healthy and happy and brown and carefree. They wouldn't be here, of course, if it wasn't for Uncle Stephen. She could never be grateful enough.

But he didn't want her to be grateful. He wanted her to be happy. Would she be happy after a while? Would she forget about Bruce? Would the ache in her throat disappear? Perhaps—if she tried very hard.

" Run along," Stephen said presently. " I want to talk to Barbara."

" Can't we hear, too? " Gay asked.

" Come on," Kit said with a scowl for Gay. " Haven't you any manners at all? "

They scattered in various directions. Barbara sat very still. What would Uncle Stephen say? " When the summer is over . . ."

It was about the house in Provincetown.

" I had a letter from the real-estate agent," Stephen said. " Someone wants to buy it."

" Oh, Uncle Stephen! " Barbara felt a strange lonely ache in her heart. She couldn't bear the thought of selling the gray-shingled house. But it had to happen sometime. . . .

" Do you mind so much? " Stephen asked, seeing

a shadow slip across her face, seeing her hands
clasping each other tightly.

"I loved it," she said with a little catch in her
voice. He couldn't know how she had loved it, the
only home she had known. She saw the willows, the
view across the harbor, the twisted apple tree, the
arbor that led to the studio. She had liked to think
it was waiting there, waiting for Bruce and for her.

"But you won't need it, probably," Stephen said.
What was she thinking? he wondered. He knew so
little about her. The summer had made no difference. She seemed more distant from him than she
had in the spring. What was she thinking? What
could he do?

"No," she agreed with a little sigh. "We won't
ever need it again."

"It's rather a good offer," Stephen continued.
"What do you want to do?"

"Sell it, I guess." It would be hers no longer,
the gray-shingled house she had loved. She wouldn't
live there with Bruce. It might just as well be sold.
"There'll be money," she added. "I can pay you
for the clothes."

"Must you?" Stephen asked, liking her independence but a little hurt as well.

"I'd feel better," she said. "That was the agree-
ment, you know."

"Yes, I know. But I'm your guardian now."

"You weren't then." She smiled faintly. "I
think that makes a difference."

Was she happy? he wondered. What lay behind the smile, behind the sadness in her eyes? She was dear to him, so very dear. Should he have waited? Should he have asked her to marry him that night beside the lily pond? She had seemed so small and so very young. Was it her mother he had kissed, the Barbara he had loved a very long time ago? He had wanted to be sure. He wasn't sure, even now.

"Would you like to go to Provincetown?" he asked.

She did not answer at once. She sat looking down at her finger-tips, her lashes curving against her cheeks.

"There are some things I would like to have." The dark lashes lifted. "The bed Father made for me, his paintings, my chest. Yes, I think I'd like to go."

"We can go next week."

"All of us?"

The question hurt Stephen a little. She didn't want to be alone with him. All summer she had clung to the children. Why?

"If you like," he agreed. "We can make it before Gay and Jamie go back to school. Is it a good idea?"

She nodded slowly, avoiding his eyes.

"Then that's settled," he said.

Suddenly she couldn't bear the thought of losing the gray-shingled house. She felt her eyes fill with tears. But she mustn't let Uncle Stephen know. She pulled herself up from the sand.

"Let's go in swimming," she said, forcing her voice to sound gay. "I'll race you, Uncle Stephen."

She ran down the beach to the edge of the curving waves. He caught up with her as she dove through a foaming breaker.

"I won!" she cried, breathless, smiling.

The tears didn't show through the water that streaked her face.

CHAPTER II

I

THE moon rose out of the ocean, making a path of silver across the waves. It shone on the cottage veranda where Stephen sat with Barbara.

"The summer is over," he said, breaking a long uneasy silence.

"Yes," she agreed. "That is the September moon."

"Have you been happy?"

"Yes," she said slowly. "I've liked it here. It's been splendid for the children."

"Do you always think first of them?"

"There are three of them," she explained, "and only one of me."

"I want you to think of yourself now," Stephen said gravely. "Don't consider the children."

There was something in his voice. What was he going to say? She sat very still, almost holding her breath.

"Would you like to go to Europe?" he asked, wishing that he could see her eyes. There was only her profile, white in the moonlight, clear as a cameo against the background of shadows.

"All of us?"

"Just you and I—and Kit, perhaps."

"Oh!" The exclamation was a soft little sound. Startled? Frightened? Happy? Stephen could not tell.

"Do I seem very old to you?" he asked. She seemed very young to him, very small and dear in the primrose colored frock.

"I don't think about your age," she said, afraid he might be hurt. She slipped her hand into his to tell him that she loved him. "I just think you're very nice."

Stephen held her hand tightly. If only he might be sure!

"Would you like to go with me—just you and I and Kit?"

She knew what he meant. She did not answer at once. It would be splendid for Kit. And Uncle Stephen was nice. Bruce had gone. Nothing else mattered at all.

"Yes," she said softly. "Yes, I would like to go."

"You know what I mean?" he asked.

"Yes, Uncle Stephen, I know."

"Will that make you happy?" he persisted. He didn't know. She sat so quietly beside him, her hand held fast in his. Wasn't she too quiet, too reasonable? What lay behind the soft notes in her voice?

"Yes," she said. She left her own chair and sat

on the arm of his, wanting to feel closer to him, afraid of the queer lonely pain in her heart. " What about Gay and Jamie? "

" We'll let them stay at school." We. It was strange to think that " we " meant Stephen and Barbara's daughter, very strange and confusing. Was she happy? He wanted to be sure.

" Are you really happy? " he asked.

" Cross my heart." She made the sign on the bodice of the primrose frock. The childish gesture touched him, and troubled him, too. Was she old enough? He thought that she was. He would be very gentle.

" We'll stay until spring," he said. " I haven't had a real vacation for years."

He had thought of it constantly during the summer. It would be easier, he had decided, to make the necessary adjustments away from home. Aunt Edith would come back to live at " Thornhedge." Gay and Jamie could be there for vacations. Aunt Edith was fond of the younger children. When they returned from Europe, Aunt Edith would have become accustomed to the idea. Mrs. Beach and her cronies would have found something else to gossip about. It seemed a sensible plan.

" Do you want to take Kit? " she asked.

" If you would like him to go." He had thought that she might be unhappy without the children. He wasn't sure that she would be content with him alone. He wasn't sure about anything, except that he wanted her to be happy. She was dearer to him than anything in the world.

" It will be splendid for Kit," she said and Stephen knew that he had judged correctly. She didn't want to be entirely alone with him. Had he misunderstood her impulsive " I do love you, Uncle Stephen! " that night beside the lily pond? But she had no interest in boys. She had discouraged them all summer, had seemed to be content with the children and him. The children and him. That, of course, was the source of his anxieties and doubts.

" Barbara," he said.

" Yes? . . ."

Her arm was around his neck. He felt her hair, silky and soft, brushing against his cheek. Barbara's hair would have felt like that—the Barbara he had loved. Why did he think of her when the younger Barbara was there beside him, close and warm and fragrant? Was it her mother he loved? It troubled him to realize that he couldn't be quite sure.

" You mustn't do this for me," he said gravely. " Or for the children. You must think of yourself."

But it didn't matter about her. Bruce had gone. The silver flute was silent, lost perhaps. It would never play again, " I love you, pretty gypsy girl with the roses in your hair." Bruce was lost, the lovely things they had planned . . .

" We'll count the stars through our skylight and every morning for breakfast I'll sing you a brand-new song."

" Bruce ! A new one every day ! "

" And a special one for Sundays."

> " —And heart-shaped gates to keep away
>   The world and all its cares
>   From one small table, dear,
>   And two small chairs. . . . "

The gates hadn't been strong enough. Bruce was gone. It hadn't been her fault or his. It was something that had happened. Uncle Stephen loved her. He had done so much for the children. She could never be grateful enough.

" I want to," she said with a little catch in her voice. " I do love you, Uncle Stephen ! "

" Darling ! " He drew her down from the arm of the chair, held her close in his arms. Doubts and uncertainties vanished while she lay there against his heart. He thought of taking her to Europe. They would revisit the village in southern France. There, with this younger Barbara, he would find the romance he had missed. She loved him, he was sure of that. She seemed content to lie against his heart.

" Darling," he said huskily. " You are dearer to me than anything in the world."

" I love *you*, Uncle Stephen," she said with a soft little quivering sigh.

Stephen did not hear the sigh. It did not seem odd to him that she called him " Uncle Stephen." His lips were against her hair, soft and silky and faintly scented.

CHAPTER III

I

THE car rolled smoothly along the Cape Cod road. Gay and Jamie, bouncing with excitement, sat on the front seat with Thomas. Stephen sat on the back seat between Barbara and Kit. They were excited, too. But they were very quiet. Stephen knew by their eyes, by their hands slipped into his, what it meant to them to be going home.

It had been raining when they left Boston. Halfway out the cape the clouds shredded themselves away, leaving patches of clear blue sky. When they reached Hyannis, the sun was shining and the sky was blue all over, as blue as a robin's egg.

"Doesn't it smell lovely?" Barbara said smiling her April smile.

"Mmm!" Kit agreed, a flush in his thin dark cheeks, his hazel eyes very bright. "I had forgotten. It smells exactly like home."

Home. . . . Barbara watched the houses skimming by, the low New England houses, the apple trees, the fence rails. It would no longer be home. The gray-shingled house at the end of the journey was to be sold. They would never come to Provincetown again. It would be easier if they didn't. Coming back was too sad.

Home was "Thornhedge" now, always and forever. Perhaps, after a while, she wouldn't mind so dreadfully. Perhaps she would be able to remember Bruce without this queer lonely feeling in her heart. When she was an old lady, perhaps. She sighed wearily. There were so many years to be lived before she would be an old lady who could remember, without pain, the far-away heartaches of youth.

Stephen heard the sigh. He glanced at her, sideways. He could not see her eyes, only the curve of her cheeks and the brown hair blowing in ringlets under her smart little hat. But there was something forlorn in her position, in the hand which he did not hold lying palm upward in her lap. He shouldn't have let her come. There were sad things to remember. Better not to go back. It hurt him when she was unhappy. He pressed her hand in a comforting way and wisely said nothing.

Barbara was grateful to him for not asking questions. He was kind and understanding. She loved him with all her heart—as she had loved Father, as she loved the children. Not as she loved Bruce. That was different. That couldn't happen again. She hoped Uncle Stephen would never know. But she couldn't look at him. Her lips were trembling so.

Gay and Jamie discovered familiar landmarks.

"There's the road to Long Nook!" Jamie shouted.

"Remember how Bruce used to take us swimming?" Gay bounced half-way around on the wide front seat. "All of us piled in his awful old car."

"It was a nice car," Kit observed, stoutly loyal to Bruce.

A lovely car, Barbara thought. She wished she might ride in it again, swooping up and down the stretch of road that was like a roller-coaster. The road to Long Nook! It was Indian summer when she saw it last, later Indian summer, sunny and hazy and golden. Her birthday. There had been sandwiches and candy with hickory nuts. She remembered it all so clearly, the clouds hiding the sky, the hut that had sheltered them from the storm. . . .

"Sing to me, Bruce. I'm frightened."

"I'll tell you a story instead."

"That will be nice."

"Once there was a gypsy boy who loved very dearly a little gypsy girl. . . ."

What was she thinking? Stephen wondered, sitting beside him so very quiet and still. Would he ever know all of her thoughts? There were times when he felt close to her and times when he felt shut out. He had no part, now, in her thoughts. What was she remembering? Her hand slipped away from his. He made no attempt to hold it.

He had no part in her thoughts. Her hand had,

unconsciously, slipped away. Every inch of the road, every tree, every house was associated with Bruce. There were the Corn Hill houses with their gaunt pointed roofs. There, after a while, was the Truro church, square and white, its steeple pricking the foliage of the trees. There was the place in the road where they had met the goose. She wondered if it had been killed and eaten. It was very precious, that goose.

There was Provincetown. They would be there very soon. Barbara's hands held each other closely. It was sad to be coming back.

The car turned from the road into Commercial Street.

"What a crazy street!" Thomas said.

A lovely street, Barbara thought. She hadn't remembered that it was so winding and friendly and quaint.

"There's Manuel's boat in the harbor!" Jamie exclaimed. "Look, 'Chips,' old man! Maybe he'll take us fishing."

The *Ariel,* too, was there, Mr. Loring's sloop, as beautiful as a dream. They could not look at that.

"It's just the same!" Kit marvelled.

Stephen laughed.

"Why shouldn't it be?" he asked. "Places seldom change in a year."

It seemed longer than that, Barbara thought. So many things had happened. But there was Miss Abbie's low white house with the dahlias ready to bloom. There was Jake Preble on his dray still wearing the same straw hat. There were the fish sheds and jutting wharves. It was dear and familiar and home.

And there, at last, was the gray-shingled house with the willow trees and the rose vine over the door.

" We're here," Kit said in a husky voice.

Barbara smiled mistily at him. She couldn't speak because of the lump in her throat.

Stephen saw her swallow, saw the tears on her lashes. He thought that, just at first, she might like to be alone.

" Get the key from the real-estate agent," he said to Thomas. " Kit will show you. Take Gay and Jamie with you."

II

Thomas and the children had gone to the real-estate agent. Stephen and Barbara were alone. She showed him the garden choked with weeds, the lilac bushes, the apple tree.

" It looks forlorn this way," she said, wanting him to love the house as she loved it. " It's nice when there aren't so many weeds."

" It's charming," Stephen said, watching Barbara. He knew that the house was dear to her. He had not known how dear. She touched, as though they were human friends, the trunks of the willows, the rose vine, the knocker shaped like an oak leaf. She peeped into the house through the windows.

"There's the old piano," she said, as though she was surprised to find it there. "It was always out of tune."

There were tears in her voice, tears misting her lashes. She smiled an April smile.

Stephen's heart swelled with tenderness.

"Darling," he said, finding, pressing her hand.

She led him beneath the arbor to the studio.

"We sat here so often," she said, pausing on the steps. She lifted the door latch. "It's open!" she said looking at Stephen in wondering surprise.

They entered the studio.

"Someone is living here!" Barbara glanced around the room. "Now who do you suppose ——"

There were signs of an occupant, a cot made up in the corner, books, a pipe, an oil stove, a battered guitar.

"How in the world ——" Stephen did not complete the question. Barbara had slipped down to the floor. She was holding the guitar against her breast, rocking it as though it were a child. "Barbara," he said, wondering, surprised.

"It's Bruce," she said through shaking sobs. "Uncle Stephen, Bruce is here!"

He understood it, then. Something died in his heart, something that never would live again.

"You love Bruce," he said slowly.

"I can't help it." She looked up at him, her face streaming with tears. "I didn't want you to know."

"That's all right." Very gently, he lifted her from the floor, settled into a chair and held her close in his arms. "It was always Bruce?" he asked.

"Yes. . . . Always," she said.

"Why didn't you tell me, dear?"

"I—I couldn't, Uncle Stephen."

"Why not?"

"Because ——" she paused, suddenly shy.

"Please," he urged, tilting her chin to look into her eyes.

"Well," she said, "at first I couldn't because we'd made so much trouble. I mean your Aunt Edith went away and Miss Emily and that was all our fault. You didn't know about children. I thought I ought to stay. And then ——" Again she paused. Her lashes, misted with tears, curved down against her cheeks.

"Then what?" Stephen asked gently. "You must tell me, dear."

"Then the night of my party—beside the lily pond. . . . I can't, Uncle Stephen." The lashes swept up from her cheeks. Her eyes were troubled and shy. "It—it seems so dreadfully hard."

"I kissed you," he said, understanding.

She nodded.

"In a different way," he continued, brushing the soft hair back from her brow.

She nodded again.

"You thought—you knew that I loved you."

Again the brown head nodded.

"And you didn't want to hurt me."

"I couldn't," she said earnestly. "You had been so kind to us all. And I do love you, Uncle Stephen." Her arms were around his neck, her cheek, damp with tears, pressed closely against his. "I love you better than anyone, except," she added, "Bruce."

"I know," Stephen said. "There are all kinds of love. I'll try to be satisfied with the kind that you can give me."

"You won't be hurt, Uncle Stephen?"

"No. I want you to be happy. You see," he said thoughtfully, "I wasn't sure ——"

"About what?"

"About you. I wasn't sure that you loved me—in a marrying way, I mean. And," he continued, "I wasn't sure about myself. I thought that I might have been kissing your mother that night by the lily pond."

"Mother?" Barbara asked.

He told her the story, then. He told her about the Barbara he had loved a very long time ago. She listened quietly, her cheek against his, the fingers of one small hand folded around his thumb.

"That's why you have Father's painting of her," she said when he had finished.

"Yes, that's why. You are very like her. I didn't know which of you I kissed that night by the

lily pond.   You see," he added, " I loved her very
much."

" Then you don't mind about Bruce? "

" I mind," he said, holding her very close.   " But
not too much.   I want you to be happy.   You are
very dear to me, Barbara, dearer than anything else
in the world."

" You're lovely! "   She smiled through the tears
on her lashes.   And then there was a change in her
face.   Her eyes widened, the flush paled out of her
cheeks.   He felt her tremble, felt the swift beating
of her heart.   " Listen," she said.

" What is it, dear? "

But he heard it then.   And he knew the song.
He had heard it very often.   .   .   .

> " *We sail the ocean blue,*
> *We catch-a da plenty-a fish.   .   .   ."*

" That's Bruce! "   Barbara slipped away from
Stephen's arms.   " He's coming, Uncle Stephen! "

III

Barbara met Bruce at the door.   Stephen saw her
hesitate, saw her expression change when she looked
at Bruce, saw her run into his arms.   He heard their
incoherent words—

" Babbie   .   .   .   Babbie, darling."

" Where were you, Bruce? "

" I went away."

"But you came back here."

"I had to find something of you."

"You've found all of me."

"For always?"

"For always. . . . Do you hear it, Bruce?"

"What, darling?"

"The silver flute."

"Funny! . . . Do you hear it, dear?"

"Yes. I haven't for ever so long. Don't let it stop playing again."

"No. . . ."

"Don't ever let it be lost."

"No. . . . Darling! I love you so much. . . ."

They had forgotten Stephen. He went out and closed the door.

CHAPTER IV

STEPHEN sat in a deck chair under the willows, looking down across the harbor, calm in the twilight, reflecting here and there the riding light of a boat. All about him was quiet. The shadows were deepening. The sound of the wind in the willows was a song that was happy and sad.

Stephen's mood harmonized with the song. He, too, was happy and sad; happy because Barbara was happy, sad because something in him had died, something which he thought would never live again. There would never be for him a real and tender romance. He had had only glimpses of it, the Barbara he had loved a very long time ago, the Barbara whom he had held, for a moment, against his heart.

The thought hurt him deeply. But under the sadness it brought there was a feeling of contentment. Such things were not for him. He had been in the cradle a sedate bachelor, gray at the temples even then. Adventure? Romance? They had no part in the pattern of his life. Some men were destined for adventure. He had been born under a quiet star.

He knew, now, why he had been troubled by

doubts and uncertainties at times during the summer. He hadn't wanted to marry Barbara. He hadn't wanted to marry Emily. He wasn't a marrying man. It was the future alone he had dreaded. He need not fear that now. There were Kit and Gay and Jamie to give his life a meaning. He would never feel entirely alone. A ready-made family was a blessing. He wasn't a marrying man. . . .

The notes of a guitar drifted through the shadows. Barbara and Bruce sat on the studio steps. Stephen could not see them but he knew they were there. Bruce was singing—

> " One small table, dear,
>   And two small chairs
> A lazy parrot for a pet
>   The kind that never swears. . . ."

Two small chairs! That was adventure, Stephen thought. They would be happy together. They were young and deeply in love. He could bear it to lose her to Bruce. Lose her? He need never lose her entirely. He had a place in her life. He knew that she would love him and remember him. That, he thought, was enough.

> " And heart-shaped gates to keep away
>   The world and all its cares
> From one small table, dear,
>   And two small chairs. . . ."

There would be cares, of course. But what did they matter? He could help them, perhaps; give them the gray-shingled house. Better not. Parents, he thought, amused at himself in the rôle of a father, meddled entirely too much. Better to let them make their own way. But he would buy the house. Sometime she might have it. . . .

"Uncle Stephen . . ." She was standing beside him, her arm linked through Bruce's arm, her eyes shining like stars.

"Yes, dear?" There was a paternal note in Stephen's voice. He was aware of it. Barbara had found for herself the proper place in his life.

"There's so much I'd like to say." She hesitated. He knew she was searching for grateful words.

"Never mind," he said.

She gave up the attempt. She left Bruce and crossed to Stephen's chair.

"I love you, Uncle Stephen," she said, her arms around his neck.

"I know." He smoothed the soft hair back from her brow.

"I—I'll always be grateful."

"I don't want you to be grateful." He held her for a moment, he held the Barbara he had loved, closely against his heart. "I want you to be happy."

"I'll do my best," Bruce said huskily.

"I'm sure of that."

"Thank you, sir."

They walked across the lawn and through the gate in the picket fence. Stephen watched them until they disappeared in the shadows. He was sad, for a moment, a sadness that had nothing to do with reason. There was in his heart for a moment a longing for the thing that was not for him. Too late, he thought, hearing above his head the happy, sad song of the willows. Too late, for always, too late. . . .

The door of the house opened. Kit came across the lawn, Gay waltzing like a butterfly, Jamie with " Chips " at his heels. They clustered about his chair. Gay's curly head dropped against his shoulder. Kit sat on the grass at his feet. Jamie hung over the chair, wanting to be close. " Chips " lapped Stephen's hand with a rough wet tongue.

" How long can we stay? " Gay asked, breaking a friendly silence.

" A day or two," Stephen answered, roughing her bright brown curls.

" Are we to live at school, Gay and I? " Jamie asked.

" I think so. Kit and I are going abroad."

" Just you and I, Uncle Stephen? " Kit looked up through the shadows with a question in his eyes. He wondered if Uncle Stephen was hurt about Bruce. He wanted to know that he wasn't.

Stephen read the question in Kit's lifted eyes. Suddenly the sadness vanished, the longing for something he could not have. They were nice youngsters. They were his. He need never feel alone.

" Yes," he said and there was a note of contentment in his voice. " We'll have to leave Barbara here, I guess. I think she wants to stay."

There's More to Follow!

More stories of the sort you like; more, probably, by the author of this one; more than 500 titles all told by writers of world-wide reputation, in the Authors' Alphabetical List which you will find on the *reverse side* of the wrapper of this book. Look it over before you lay it aside. There are books here you are sure to want—some, possibly, that you have *always* wanted.

It is a *selected* list; every book in it has achieved a certain measure of *success.*

The Grosset & Dunlap list is not only the greatest Index of Good Fiction available, it represents in addition a generally accepted Standard of Value. It will pay you to

Look on the Other Side of the Wrapper!

In case the wrapper is lost write to the publishers for a complete catalog

ROMANCES OF THE MODERN GIRL

Here is a list of books by well known writers of romance stories for the modern girl. They are writers whose names have become famous with the publication of their stories as newspaper serials. These books are now available in the Grosset & Dunlap Edition.

ROB EDEN
Pay Check
Heartbreak Girl
Second Choice
Loot
Dancing Feet
$20 a Week
The Girl with Red Hair

BEATRICE BURTON
Mary Faith
Lovejoy
Easy
Money Love
The Flapper Wife

ALMA SIOUX SCARBERRY
Flighty
High Hat
Dimpled Racketeer
Make-Up

EDNA ROBB WEBSTER
Joretta
Lipstick Girl
Love, Preferred

ANNE GARDNER
Masquerade
Working Wives

ROBERT D. ANDREWS
Three Girls Lost
One Girl Found

MABEL McELLIOTT
Love Feud
The Man Hunters

HAZEL ROSS HAILEY
Lure

CLAIRE POMEROY
Golden Youth

VIDA HURST
No Such Girl
Glittering Sham
Honeymoon Limited
One Man Woman
Blind Date
Marriage a la Mode
Big Game

MAY CHRISTIE
Playgirls in Love
The High Speed Girl
Flirting Wives
A Kiss For Corinna
Love's Ecstasy

ELENORE MEHERIN
Chickie
Chickie, A Sequel
Sandy
Nora Lee
Jerry

RUTH DEWEY GROVES
The Husband Hunter
Heartache
When a Girl Loves

LAURA LOU BROOKMAN
Leap Year Bride
Guilty Lips

VERNIE E. CONNELLY
Runaway Wife
Alimony Queens

CLARE SHARPE HOUGH
The Charming Cheat

JOAN CLAYTON
One Girl's Morals

ELEANOR EARLY
Love's Denial

GROSSET & DUNLAP, Publishers, NEW YORK